T0353226

Bello
hidden talent rediscovered

Bello is a digital-only imprint of Pan Macmillan,
established to breathe new life into previously published,
classic books.

At Bello we believe in the timeless power of the imagination,
of a good story, narrative and entertainment, and we want to
use digital technology to ensure that many more readers
can enjoy these books into the future.

We publish in ebook and print-on-demand formats
to bring these wonderful books to new audiences.

www.panmacmillan.com/imprint-publishers/bello

Jocelyn Brooke

Jocelyn Brooke was born in 1908 on the south coast, and took to the educational process with reluctance. He contrived to run away from public school twice within a fortnight, but then settled, to his own mild surprise, at Bedales before going to Worcester College, Oxford, where his career as an undergraduate was unspectacular. He worked in London for a while, then in the family wine-merchants in Folkestone, but this and other ventures proved variously unsatisfactory.

In 1939, Brooke enlisted in the Royal Army Medical Corps, and reenlisted after the war as a Regular: 'Soldiering,' he wrote, 'had become a habit.' The critical success of *The Military Orchid* (1948), the first volume of his Orchid trilogy, provided the opportunity to buy himself out, and he immediately settled down to write, publishing some fifteen titles between 1948 and 1955, including the successive volumes of the trilogy, *A Mine of Serpents* (1949) and *The Goose Cathedral* (1950). His other published work includes two volumes of poetry, *December Spring* (1946) and *The Elements of Death* (1952), the novels *The Image of a Drawn Sword* (1950) and *The Dog at Clambercrown* (1955), as well as some technical works on botany.

Jocelyn Brooke died in 1966.

Jocelyn Brooke

CONVENTIONAL WEAPONS

First published in 1961 by Faber and Faber Limited

This edition published 2017 by Bello
an imprint of Pan Macmillan
20 New Wharf Road, London N1 9RR
Associated companies throughout the world

www.panmacmillan.com/imprint-publishers/bello

ISBN 978-1-5098-5588-9 EPUB
ISBN 978-1-5098-5587-2 PB

Typeset by Ellipsis, Glasgow

Visit **www.panmacmillan.com** to read more about all our books
and to buy them. You will also find features, author interviews and
news of any author events, and you can sign up for e-newsletters
so that you're always first to hear about our new releases.

Encounter in Valetta

I noticed him first in the street, standing on the pavement edge waiting to cross: a big man in his fifties, going bald, with the beginnings of a paunch, and an expression upon his fleshy face of habitual ill-temper. The face was immediately familiar: something about that square, flattened forehead, the firm jut of the chin, suggested somebody whom, long ago, I had known fairly well and—I felt pretty sure—disliked; some schoolfellow, perhaps, aged beyond recognition, or someone I had known at Oxford, or in the Army. He wore a grey alpaca coat, flannel trousers and an old school or club tie which I couldn't identify. As I passed him on the pavement, his glance, for an instant, met mine, but the eyes— blue-grey, stern and curiously opaque—gave no hint of recognition.

The street was Kingsway, the town Valetta, where I had come for a late-summer holiday, and just now I was on my way to cash a cheque at Barclay's Bank. I paused on the steps of the building and glanced, once again, at the man on the pavement: I was positive that I knew him; but what was his name, where and when had I met him before? Presently there was a lull in the traffic, and I saw him make off, with a jaunty, athletic stride, across the street; soon he was lost to view among the crowd on the opposite pavement.

I cashed my cheque, and emerged again, a few minutes later, into the ferocious noonday sun. The day was hot even for a Maltese September, and my thoughts were centred upon a drink before lunch; yet the big man's face, so briefly seen and so instantly familiar, continued to haunt me, and I dawdled up the torrid street, peering into the bars and shops in the hope of seeing him again. The impression that I had, in the past, had cause to dislike him, persisted; something in his stern glance, as our eyes met, had recalled the brutish, implacable hostility of an elder boy at school by whom I had been habitually persecuted; or was I, after all, thinking of some officer or N.C.O. who, at some forgotten period during my Army days, had made my life a misery? In middle age such "institutional" memories tend to become confused: schooldays and soldiering merge into a multiple symbol of authority, the fifth-form bully becomes indistinguishable from the drill-sergeant, the school playing-fields from the barrack-square.

Whoever he was, the man was no longer to be seen, and at last, with a curious feeling of frustration, I turned into a bar for a glass of beer. It wasn't that I specially wanted to scrape acquaintance with him, but that half-remembered countenance had set up an irritating echo in my mind, which refused to be silenced. I was convinced—unreasonably enough—that if only I could catch another glimpse of him I should at once remember his name and the forgotten background of our past relationship. Such an encounter was, however, unlikely; I was leaving Valetta tomorrow for the smaller island of Gozo, and the man was in all probability a mere bird of passage, spending a day or two in Malta on his way elsewhere.

I spent that afternoon bathing at Mellieha, and in the evening, unable to face the horrors of Maltese cookery, decided to give myself a treat and dine at the one decent hotel in the island. This was a big, brand-new barrack of a place, catering with a somewhat blatant exclusiveness for the officer-class and the Anglo-Maltese aristocracy; I didn't like it, but at least it would be comfortable and relatively cool, and the food was good.

By now I had almost forgotten my encounter of the morning, and it came as a slight shock, when I entered the hotel cocktail-bar, to be confronted once again by the man himself. For the second time that day I was aware of an instantaneous sense of recognition, though I still couldn't remember the man's name, or when and where I had known him. He was sitting by himself at a small table in a corner and scowling, as unamiably as ever, across the crowded room. As I bought myself a drink at the bar I noticed that he kept glancing anxiously towards the door, as though he were expecting somebody.

Tired after my bathe, I was determined to sit down, but the room was packed, and at first I could see nowhere to sit; then I noticed that there was an empty chair at the big man's table, half-hidden behind a pillar. Steering a zigzag course through a jostling crowd of officers, I made my way resolutely towards it.

"Excuse me," I said, "but is anybody using this chair?"

"Sit down if you like," he rapped out brusquely, glancing up at me with a look of barely concealed hostility. "I *am* expecting someone, as it happens, but he's not turned up yet."

At any other time, I might have taken the hint, but just now I was far too tired to be tactful, and sat down in the vacant chair. As I did so, the man rather pointedly turned his face away, and shifted his own chair, with what seemed a calculated offensiveness, farther from mine.

I had taken off my coat and draped it over the chair-back, but even so I found the stuffy heat of the room almost unbearable. Soon I ordered another drink, and as I did so, saw that my companion was regarding me with morose disapproval. Suddenly, to my surprise, he leaned forward and addressed me.

"You'll excuse my mentioning it," he said, in brusque, orderly-room tones, "but I'd advise you to put your coat on."

"Put my coat on?" I queried stupidly.

"Yes, they rather expect it here in the evenings."

"But that's nonsense, in weather like this," I retorted rather sharply.

With a quick, irritable movement, he flexed his wrist and looked at his watch.

"Sorry, old boy—coats on after seven. It's a regulation here. No business of mine, of course, but I thought I'd warn you, that's all."

I stared at him in astonishment: irritated not so much by the absurd regulation as by his own insolent assumption of authority.

"But damn it all," I exploded, my nerves frayed by the heat and the overcharged atmosphere, "it must be at least a hundred and twenty in this room at the moment."

"The drill's the same, whatever the temperature, I'm afraid," he snapped.

We glared at each other, with mutual hostility, across the table. I was tired and on edge, and felt quite capable of losing my temper. As for my companion, I could see that he too was controlling himself with difficulty: his hand trembled as he lifted his glass, and I guessed that he was already slightly drunk. Suddenly he gave vent to a curious sound, half-way between a grunt and a chuckle.

"All right, old boy—have it your own way. Only don't say I didn't warn you." He stared at me over his glass, his eyes dark with some private vexation which was, I felt, only incidentally connected with myself and my *outré* behaviour; and once again the vivid sense of some shared past made me rack my brains in the effort to recall his name and identity. The school bully at St. Ethelbert's? Some jack-in-office at Netley or Boyce Barracks? His voice, no less than his features, seemed half-familiar: clipped, rather hoarse and almost aggressively "public-school", with a curious overtone of exacerbation, a hint of some deep-seated and habitual resentment. I watched him lift his glass again, and could see that he was still keeping his temper with difficulty. Prudently, I remained silent; then, to my surprise, he turned and spoke to me again.

"You Army?" he shot at me, abruptly.

I shook my head.

"Navy, then, eh?"

"No, no—I'm just over here for a holiday."

"Queer place to come for a holiday, isn't it?"

I explained, briefly, that I had blued my currency allowance in France, earlier in the year, and wanted some sun before the summer was over.

"Oh well, of course, Malta's sterling area and all that, but most people find it a bit stuffy at this season."

"I happen to like the heat," I said.

He grunted, discouragingly, and once again fixed his eyes upon the door; half-turned away from me, he quite obviously wished to convey that our conversation was now at an end. Impelled partly by sheer curiosity, partly by a mischievous desire to penetrate his defences, I said at last:

"I gather you live out here?"

He turned abruptly towards me, with an arrogant tilt of his head.

"Yes, as a matter of fact I do," he replied curtly.

"I suppose you've got some job here?"

I noticed an angry glint come into his eyes; for two pins, I thought, he would have ordered me, sharply, to mind my own business.

"No, no," he said with a rather edgy politeness, "I've retired. I live out here because it's cheaper—practically no income tax, you see."

"What do you do with yourself most of the time?" I asked, curiously.

He glanced away, evasively.

"Oh, I keep myself occupied—swimming and all that. Used to play a bit of polo, but can't afford it nowadays. Got a bit of a garden, too—my wife's a very keen gardener. Good thing, that—gives her something to do. She's not too keen on the social life, and nor am I."

He signalled to the waiter, ordered a drink, then pointed to my glass.

"What's your poison?" he barked at me.

"Er—thanks very much, I'll have a whisky," I said, taken by surprise, and a moment later wished I had said no.

He gave me a quick grin which made his face seem, for a moment, almost boyish; though it remained (I thought) the face of an unusually disgruntled and ill-tempered boy.

"Awful pub this, really—I don't use it much myself," he said. "Fact is, I'm meeting a son of mine, he's in for a couple of nights on his way to Cyprus. Can't think what's happened to him—he said he'd 'phone if he got held up."

"He's in the Army, is he?" I asked, without much interest.

"Yes, West Kents—my old mob, as it happens. His battalion's been ordered to Famagusta."

I pricked up my ears: surely I had known somebody, once, in the West Kents?

The drinks arrived.

"Well, cheerioh, here's mud in your eye."

I lifted my glass.

"Fact is, I don't really drink a lot out here—not normally," he said, in a bluff, man-to-man tone which struck me as rather unconvincing. "Just an occasional binge, you know—I find the old liver begins to play me up, otherwise. Trouble is, it's a whole-time job keeping fit in this climate—I manage to get a swim most days, play a bit of squash, too, but it's a damned unhealthy spot. I was getting a bit of a pot on me, about a year ago, but I've lost nearly a stone and a half since then, I'm glad to say."

Once again I was struck by something familiar in his tone of truculent *bonhomie*; and his obsessive concern with physical fitness—that, too, seemed to fit into the picture. Made suddenly bold by the whisky, I decided to clear up, once and for all, the mystery of his identity.

"It's a funny thing, you know," I said casually, "but I've a feeling I've met you somewhere before."

He gave me a curious look: startled, suspicious, almost shifty—the face, I thought, of the sahib on the run.

"Can't say I've any recollection of it. Fact is, I've been living out here ever since the war: only been home twice in the last ten years."

"It was longer than that, I fancy."

"You weren't in the West Kents by any chance?"

"No, I was R.A.M.C."

"Oh, you're a doctor, then?"

"No, no—I was only a private."

"A private, eh?" he echoed, with a hint of disdain.

One might have guessed, I thought with amusement, that he would hold old-fashioned views about "gentleman rankers".

Just at that moment my ear was caught by the voice of a waiter paging somebody in the crowd. For a moment I didn't catch the name; then, as the man drew nearer, his words rang out plangently above the confused ground-bass of talk and laughter:

"Major Tufnell-Greene! Major Tufnell-*Gre*-eene!"

The name struck me with a sudden shock of familiarity: I had once known some Tufnell-Greenes in my youth—they were, in fact, distant cousins of mine.

Then I saw my companion lurch, a little unsteadily, to his feet.

"Someone looking for me?" he asked.

"Major Tufnell-Greene, sir? You are wanted on the telephone, pleess."

"O.K., I'll be out in a sec." He finished his drink at a gulp, and gave a nod in my direction. " 'Scuse me, won't you? I expect it's that lad of mine. Be back in two shakes of a duck's arse."

I rose impulsively from my chair: the penny had dropped at last.

"Good gracious," I exclaimed, "you must be *Geoffrey* Greene——"

But I was too late: he was already out of earshot, pushing his way, impatiently and none too gently, through the crowd towards the door.

The penny had dropped; yet I felt my momentary excitement give way, almost immediately, to a sense of flatness and anticlimax. So that, I thought, sinking back into my chair, was that: the man whose identity had so puzzled me was merely Geoffrey Greene—a bore whom I had all but forgotten, and with whom I was not in the least anxious to renew my acquaintance. Even the school bully or the drill-sergeant, I thought disconsolately, would have been almost preferable.

It seemed extraordinary that I shouldn't have recognized him: he had changed, certainly, in the twenty years or so since we had last met, though not so much as one might have expected. The face—lined and coarsened as it was—the hectoring voice, the brusque, impatient gestures, all could now be fitted into the remembered picture of Geoffrey Greene as I had known him; so too, for that matter, could his evasive air, the hint of shiftiness in his eyes when I had questioned him. Yet perhaps, after all (I thought), it wasn't so odd that I should have forgotten him. Old friends and distant kinsfolk of my father's, the Tufnell-Greenes had meant little enough in my life, even at that period—a quarter of a century ago—when I had known them best. My relations with them had been, for the most part, of that artificial kind which is imposed by the mere accident of kinship or propinquity, and which, impinging only upon the mind's surface, strikes but the shallowest of roots in one's memory. I remembered the Greenes, in fact, much as one remembers the characters in some dull novel which one has never bothered to finish.

In the past I had disliked Geoffrey, and for some reason my vague memories of him as a young man were tinged with a sense of humiliation for which, at the moment, I couldn't account. With his younger brother, Nigel, I had been on somewhat friendlier terms, though he, like Geoffrey himself, had long since passed out of my life. I wondered, vaguely, what had happened to him: the family black sheep, unhappy, ineffectual and always in trouble. Probably he was dead—indeed, I seemed to remember hearing of his death during the war. Or was I confusing him with someone else?

I looked at my watch: it was already ten minutes since Geoffrey had left the bar. Surely no telephone call could have taken as long as that.

Just then the waiter, whom I had noticed hovering near my table, leaned forward discreetly and addressed me.

"I must ask you, sir, pleess to put on your coat."

"Why?" I asked bluntly.

"Pleess, it is after seven o'clock."

I should have liked to proclaim—however ineffectually—my disdain for colonial etiquette by marching straight out of the bar; the thought of dinner at my own cheap hotel was enough, however, to cow me into submission. Meekly I put on my coat and continued to sip my whisky. There wasn't really much point in waiting for Geoffrey; having at last identified him, I felt nothing but boredom at the prospect of his company. Yet I remained, perversely, rooted firmly in my chair, sweating uncomfortably in my tweed coat. The truth was that, being unattached and lonely, I would have welcomed the society of almost anybody at that moment, however tedious and unrewarding.

Another ten minutes passed: it was almost certain, by now, that Geoffrey wouldn't be coming back. Probably his son had suggested some other meeting-place, and Geoffrey had long since left the hotel to join him. By now it was past eight o'clock, and I was extremely hungry; yet I continued to wait, lingering over my drink, and speculating vaguely as to the later chapters of the Greene saga—that unfinished Galsworthian novel whose very existence, until a few minutes ago, I had all but forgotten. My memories of the Greenes, after twenty years, had become singularly dim: during that time, I had lost touch with plenty of old friends, but I did at least remember most of them fairly clearly, whereas the Greenes, when I tried to recall them, remained unfocused and scarcely differentiated, mere figures in a landscape—and (I thought) a pretty dull landscape at that.

Only Nigel emerged with a certain clarity: I had, after all, known him fairly well, and it was odd (if he were still alive) that he should have vanished from the scene so completely. Nor, since the war, had I heard anything of his wife, with whom I had been on rather closer terms of friendship, at one time, than with Nigel himself. And what, I wondered, had induced Geoffrey to settle in Malta? He had scarcely sounded enthusiastic about the island; and Madge, his wife—from a remark he had let fall—appeared to be something of a recluse, devoted to gardening, which from what I remembered of her seemed oddly out of character. And why had she not come to the hotel with Geoffrey to meet their son?

I finished my drink at last, and walked out of the bar; in the foyer, on my way to the dining-room, I stopped to have a word with the hall-porter.

No, he said, in answer to my question, Major Tufnell-Greene was no longer in the hotel.

"He left about an hour ago, sir—I got him a taxi. He was called to the 'phone just before—seemed in a hurry to be off, like. Could I give him any message, sir?"

"Is he staying here, then?"

"No sir, he's not staying in the hotel."

"You'll be seeing him again, though, will you?"

"Oh yes, sir, he's sure to be in again sometime—him and Mrs. Greene, they comes in quite a bit, being residents, like. No message I could give?"

"No, it doesn't matter."

"Thank you very much, sir" (as I slipped a shilling into his hand). "Major Greene's a friend of yours, is he, sir?"

"I used to know him years ago," I said. "In fact, he's some sort of cousin of mine."

"Is he really, sir? Then I daresay you knew his brother—quite a celebrity in his way, I believe."

"D'you mean *Nigel*?" I exclaimed in astonishment.

"I'm not quite sure of the name, sir, but I've heard he wrote books."

"He wrote *books*?"

"That's right, sir."

"What sort of books?" I asked, aware that the porter was looking at me with a certain scepticism—as well he might, for it must have struck him as odd, to say the least, that I should display such ignorance about a family with whom I had claimed acquaintance and even kinship.

"I couldn't rightly say what sort of books, sir, but I've often heard Mrs. Greene speak of them."

"He's dead, is he?" I asked—for I had noticed that he spoke of Nigel in the past tense.

The porter's face took on a suitably obituary look.

"Oh yes, sir. It must be—let me see, now—getting on for ten years ago. Just after we opened, that would be . . . Excuse me, sir—" he turned aside, apologetically but firmly, to attend to a party of new arrivals, laden with baggage, who had just entered through the swing-doors.

Reluctantly, I made way for them; the porter seemed likely to be occupied for some time, and in any case I wanted my dinner. Perhaps, after all, I thought, we had been speaking at cross-purposes, and the porter had been referring to some other family of the same name; yet it seemed unlikely, to say the least, that two Major Tufnell-Greenes should have left the hotel simultaneously half an hour ago. Yet who—if the porter had really been speaking of Geoffrey—was the brother who wrote books, and who was "something of a celebrity"? It couldn't be Nigel: if Nigel had ever written a book (which was highly unlikely anyway) I should most certainly have heard of it; and Geoffrey had had no other brothers.

The more I thought about it, the more puzzling it seemed; after dinner, I thought, I would talk to the porter again, and try to get things clear.

But when, an hour or so later, I returned to the foyer, the man I had spoken to had gone off duty. The night-porter, who had replaced him, was less well-informed.

"Major Greene, sir? Would that be the young chap with a fair moustache, in the Engineers?"

"No, no—Major *Tufnell*-Greene: he lives out here, he's retired."

"Ah, now I get you, sir—big busty bloke, got a house at Mdina."

"That would be the one, I expect. D'you know him pretty well?"

"Oh yes, sir, I know him quite well. And Mrs. Greene too."

"A tall, thinnish lady?" I prompted him.

The porter gave a puzzled frown and shook his head.

"No, sir—I'd not call Mrs. Greene a tall lady, nor not exactly thin, neither. I'd describe her as a rather short lady—short and, well, stoutish you might say. Black hair, going a bit grey."

Once again we seemed at cross-purposes: the man was obviously confusing Geoffrey's wife with someone else, for Madge had been tall, blonde and of the skinny type which seldom runs to fat.

"You didn't know the Major's younger brother, I suppose—the one who died?"

"No, sir, I can't say I remember the Major having a brother. That'd be before my time, I daresay—I've only been here just on two years,"

"I mean the one who wrote books," I added hopefully.

"Wrote books, did he, sir? No, I can't say I recollect him at all, sir."

I gave him a shilling: this particular *recherche du temps perdu*

11

was coming a bit expensive, I thought, as I passed through the swing-doors into the bright-lit, torrid night. One or other of the two porters must certainly have been talking through his hat: probably both. Not only had Nigel become a literary celebrity, but Geoffrey had now acquired a short, stoutish wife. The facts simply didn't fit, and I began to wonder, rather wildly, whether the man I had met in the bar had really been Geoffrey Greene at all.

The mystery—as such things will—continued to nag at my mind with an irritating persistence; little though I cared about the Greenes, I couldn't get them out of my mind, and I was particularly baffled—and somewhat intrigued—by the brother who "wrote books". I made my way leisurely towards the centre of the town, glancing into the bars and cafés as I passed, half-hoping that I might run into Geoffrey and his son. The last thing I wanted was to get seriously involved with them; on the other hand I did, very much, want to clear up the mystery. Moreover, it would be quite amusing to introduce myself: doubtless Geoffrey would be surprised—and perhaps not too pleasantly—to learn that he was united by ties of blood to the coatless and inquisitive ex-private who had shared his table in the bar; and I did, after all (I suddenly remembered), owe him a drink.

I wandered round the town for an hour or so, looking in at a series of mainly rather nasty bars and cafés, but my quarry continued to elude me. At last, feeling tired, I sat down in the big open-air café at the bottom of Kingsway. Lingering over my last drink, I watched the thinning crowds strolling beneath the trees, and wondered why I should have wasted a whole evening in pursuing a man for whom I felt nothing but a bored dislike. By now I had ceased to feel much interest even in the anomalous figures of Geoffrey's literary brother and his fat wife. Tomorrow I left for Gozo, and in a fortnight's time should be returning to England: it was highly unlikely that I should ever see Geoffrey again, nor (I decided) did I care two hoots either way.

By the morning I had almost entirely forgotten my encounter with Geoffrey, and it is likely enough that I should never have given the Greenes another thought, but for a trifling accident. As I was washing before breakfast, my cake of soap happened to slither from my hand on to the floor, and, as I bent to pick it up, its oval, brownish shape seemed suddenly fraught with a mysterious and compulsive significance. It was a perfectly ordinary cake of soap, which I had bought at a chemist's in Valetta a day or two before; yet now, holding it in my hand, its sweetish smell and the sticky feel of the lather evoked for me some vague, amorphous memory which, though it refused as yet to click into focus, I knew to be closely associated in some way with the Greenes. But how? Why on earth, I asked myself, standing there in front of the washstand, should I connect the Greenes with a cake of soap? Cudgel my brains as I would, I was totally unable—while I brushed my teeth, shaved and put on my clothes—to establish the missing link; the soap, like the famous group of trees near Balbec, continued to withhold its secret.

And then, all at once, I remembered: and felt the thrill of the archaeologist who, lighting upon some fragment of pottery or mosaic, recognizes the essential clue which will enable him to reconstruct the architecture, the language and the social institutions of some long-buried and forgotten culture. The Greenes—those characters in an unfinished middle-brow novel about whom, on the previous evening, I had been able to remember next to nothing—leapt into sudden life, like dimly-seen figures upon a stage who step into the glare of the spotlight; and the vague, unseizable memories which had flickered so inconsequently through my mind fell instantly into focus, radiating outwards, like iron filings within a magnet's orbit, from the central and vividly-perceived image of a cake of soap: not, indeed, the one with which I had just washed myself, but another, such as I had not seen for many years; a *green* soap, with a pleasant, tangy odour suggestive of seaweed, which in my childhood we used to buy from Mr. Timms, the chemist in Sandgate.

CHAPTER ONE

The Name of Greene

Mr. Timms's soap was a rather special brand, supposed to be adapted to the hardness of the local water; dark green and translucent, smelling of the sea, the oval, slippery tablets embodied for me the quintessential idea of greenness, so that when I heard my parents talking about one or another of the Greene family, I tended to envisage a personage at once luminous and darkly verdant, flecked with a peculiarly thin, glairy lather and exhaling the slightly putrescent aroma of the beach at low tide.

The name of Greene—thus tinged, by association, with a saponaceous quality from which, to this day, I find some difficulty in separating it—haunted my childhood, recurring intermittently in the course of those diffuse and mainly unintelligible grown-up conversations upon which I would eavesdrop with the strained yet hopeful attention that one brings to bear upon a play in some foreign language of which one has scarcely, as yet, acquired the rudiments. The Greenes, I had good reason for supposing, were a real family, with whom my parents were acquainted, and with whom, even, they sometimes went to stay; yet since I never saw them myself, and was therefore unable to form any but the vaguest idea of what they looked like, they remained for me largely mythical: a multiple entity, protean, hydra-headed and having about as much relation to real life as the characters in a fairy tale.

The Greenes, in fact, were for me no more than a legend, but a legend which, nevertheless, became part of the fabric of my life. Debarred though I was, by lack of any detailed information, from building up an authentic picture of them as real people, I was at least able, by judicious eavesdropping, to evolve a lively and extensive mythology of the Greene family: Olympian figures who, though far removed from the mortal world which I inhabited, did possess certain characteristics which could be apprehended in human terms. They were, for instance, immensely rich: in any conversation which referred to them, this fact was almost bound to be mentioned. They were also said to be snobs; I didn't know what this word meant, and asked one of the maids, who told me that a snob was the same as a cobbler. The Greenes, then, I supposed, must be people who repaired shoes, though I was still puzzled as to why they should be so often referred to as *terrible* snobs, as though to be a cobbler were in some way wicked, though at the same time rather laughable. For the Greenes, though so rich and grand, and in general so worthy of respect, tended to be referred to, more especially by my mother, with a certain humorous disdain. There was, in fact, something mysteriously *funny* about the Greenes; even my father would sometimes poke a little mild fun at them though, since they were his blood-relations, he was restrained by a sense of family loyalty from the cruder jibes which these "snobs" were apt to call forth from my mother and, on occasion, from my maternal aunts and uncles.

Another unpleasant characteristic of the Greenes was, apparently, that they smelt: one of my uncles, who knew the family well, once declared in my hearing that they "stank in his nostrils". I had also gathered that the Greene family was an enormous one: they swarmed, they pullulated, their various branches and offshoots were scattered widely over the home counties and farther afield; thus, there were the Richard Greenes in Suffolk, the Walter Greenes in Surrey, the Herbert Greenes at Blackheath, and many more. All the Greenes, moreover, were excessively philoprogenitive: every one of them, according to my mother, had "fids of children". If their wives (or husbands) died, they promptly married again, and continued busily to reproduce themselves. This notable fertility, I thought, probably accounted for the fact—which had rather puzzled me—that the Greenes were sometimes referred to, in our family circle, as being "common". As an amateur botanist, I associated the word chiefly with plants which were so described in the floras, and which, like the Greenes themselves, had the power of dispersing their seed prolifically and over a wide area. The Greene family, in fact, I envisaged as being rather like the *Cruciferae* or the Composites, dull and undistinguished by comparison with such floral aristocrats as the *Liliaceae* or the noble tribe of orchids.

It was when I was about six years old—at the beginning of the First World War—that my purely mythological conception of the Greenes became incarnated in a more fleshly mould. One day I was told that a little boy, a cousin called Nigel Greene, was coming to stay with us; he was to be left in our charge for a fortnight, while his mother stayed with relations in the neighbourhood. I was prejudiced against him from the start, for in my experience little-boys-who-came-to-stay were almost certain to be in one way or another unacceptable. Either they were older than myself, and I was bullied, or they were younger, and I was bored. Nigel, it appeared, was a year older than myself, so would, I presumed, come under the bullying category. I was also given to understand that he was extremely spoilt and very naughty, and I lived through the days which preceded his arrival in a state of acute nervous apprehension.

Nigel, in due course, arrived, and at once my worst fears were confirmed. He wore a sailor-suit, with "H.M.S. Dreadnought" in gold letters on the hat-band, and this in itself was enough to disturb me profoundly. A thin, lanky child, with a mop of fair but rather mousy hair, he peered short-sightedly about him with an air of chronic resentment. On the very first day, at tea, he behaved so badly—snatching at his food, dropping it on the floor, refusing to say please or thank you—that he had to be removed to the nursery.

"He's tired after the journey," my nurse charitably commented, but this comforting theory was quickly to be disproved in the days which followed.

Nigel's behaviour could only be described as manic-depressive, alternating as it did between fits of the sullens and outbreaks of sudden, terrifying violence. He teased the maids, maltreated the cat and trampled on the garden beds; if admonished, he would lose his temper, bursting into tears and screaming as loud as he could. I was vividly reminded of naughty Frederick in *Struwwelpeter*, and half-expected some dire calamity to overwhelm our guest, but no such gratifying consequence occurred.

I was shocked and frightened by Nigel's behaviour, but to my relief he made no attempt to persecute me; for the most part, indeed, he left me severely alone. He suffered from recurrent headaches, and these my nurse attributed—probably correctly—to his bad eyesight; it was even debated whether he should be sent to an oculist, but this was felt by my parents to be an unnecessary assumption of responsibility.

More than anything else, I found Nigel a bore: he shared none of my interests, and his only hobby seemed to be the collecting of Army badges, of which he possessed quite a number, though their real value for him lay chiefly in their association with his elder brother, Geoffrey, who was almost grown-up, and would soon, it seemed, be a soldier himself. Nigel idolized his brother, yet obviously lived in terror of him. My nurse, provoked beyond bearing, would sometimes threaten to inform his parents of Nigel's misdeeds—a stratagem wholly without effect; but a similar threat to "tell Geoffrey" would—as she soon discovered—produce an immediate (if only temporary) abatement of his naughtiness. On the other hand, he never tired of singing his brother's praises, and would relate innumerable and very boring anecdotes of Geoffrey's enormous strength, his prowess at games, and so forth. So obsessed did he seem, indeed, by this proto-fascist hero-cult, that my mother was inclined to deplore his feeling for Geoffrey as being, ever so slightly, "morbid".

Meanwhile, despite all my nurse's threats, he continued to be as naughty as ever. There was something curiously wanton and deliberate about his misbehaviour: it was as though he positively enjoyed courting disaster, if only to see just how far he could go without actually incurring it. My parents were in a difficult position, for it is a delicate business to punish other people's children, and I suspect that Nigel, slyly aware of his advantage, was determined to make the most of it.

*

17

The fortnight which Nigel spent at Sandgate seemed endless, but eventually Mrs. Greene arrived back from her visit to her cousins at Tenterden, and on the day following Geoffrey, who had been at an O.T.C. camp in Sussex, came to join us for two nights before returning, with Nigel and his mother, to their home at Blackheath.

My first encounter with the famous Geoffrey was entirely disastrous. For some reason which I forget, it had been arranged that my nurse and myself should meet his train, with a cab, at Shorncliffe station. My nurse was a little worried—since he had never visited us before—as to how we should recognize him; few passengers, however, left the train at Shorncliffe, and it was impossible to mistake the haughty young gentleman of sixteen (he seemed to me a great deal older) who stepped from a second-class carriage carrying a cricket-bag, a tennis-racquet and a fishing-rod, and attended by a large and rather fierce-looking bull-terrier. I was aware of dark eyebrows beneath a square, box-like forehead, a straight nose, a stern though full-lipped mouth and black, close-cropped hair. He wore a school blazer and flannel trousers cut rather short in the fashion of the day, so as to reveal socks of a notably loud pattern, with clocks. He looked alarmingly smart and self-possessed, and I detested him at sight.

He greeted us with an air of aloof condescension; the next moment, he was fussing over his luggage in the guard's van, and issuing short, sharp commands to the slow-moving and somewhat dull-witted porter. His voice must have broken early, for he spoke in a deep, rather harsh baritone. At last he rejoined us, and his smaller luggage (together with the bull-terrier) was piled into the cab; the rest was left for later delivery, and consisted, I seem to remember, of an enormous trunk, besides several smaller suitcases, a school playbox and a bag of golf clubs (it should be remembered that no middle-class person in those days—not even a schoolboy— ever travelled with very much less). Installed in the cab, and jog-trotting along Coolinge Lane towards Sandgate, I began to feel very unwell; perhaps it was the weather (it was August, and very hot), or possibly the excitement engendered by Geoffrey's arrival; at all events, suddenly and without warning, I was violently sick—

all over Geoffrey's beautifully creased trousers and his smart coloured socks.

To do him justice, he behaved very well: he was impeccably polite, though one sensed that only an iron self-control prevented him from a violent and probably destructive explosion of wrath. As for myself, I had never in my life felt so mortified; true, I had taken an immediate dislike to Geoffrey, but Nigel's elaborate build-up had not been without its effect, and my own feelings about him had, by this time, acquired a certain quality of ambivalence. I wanted, at all costs, to produce a good impression upon this athletic paragon, and now, already, I was aware that he must—and with every justification—loathe and despise me.

Most of Geoffrey's time, during his short visit, was spent on the beach, bathing and disporting himself in a canoe with my brother, who had now also returned for the holidays. Nigel, owing to some minor tummy upset, was not allowed to bathe, but would sit spellbound upon the shingle, watching with adoring eyes the aquatic feats of his hero. Hating the sea myself, I would remain in hiding, half-way up the garden; from here I would contemplate Geoffrey's antics with a kind of perverse fascination: hating him for his self-importance and his aggressive heartiness, yet deriving a masochistic thrill from the very qualities which I professed to despise.

But if Geoffrey had incurred my dislike, he was none too popular with the rest of the household. For a boy of his age, he threw his weight about to a degree which seemed, to my family, excessive. His innumerable possessions littered the house, one was perpetually falling over cricket-bats or tennis-racquets, and the bull-terrier was both ubiquitous and bad-tempered, snapping at anybody who tried to restrain him, and fighting with our black Pomeranian, Pompey. At meal times, Geoffrey would dominate the conversation, lecturing us about his doings at Uppingham, about his O.T.C. camp, and even—for this was the summer of 1914—about the progress of the war. He was in the Army class, and hoped soon to pass into Sandhurst; he was inflamed by the prospect of killing Germans, and though this was considered an unexceptionable ambition for a schoolboy in 1914, there was an obsessive, gloating quality about

Geoffrey's blood-lust which caused my mother, once again, to employ the word "morbid". His manners—apart from his over-talkativeness—were fairly good, in a stiff, conventional way, yet there was a truculent, domineering strain in him which no amount of good manners could wholly conceal. On more than one occasion my father was observed to be "looking down his nose", an action which denoted his strongest disapproval and which, in our family circle, was held to be equivalent to a sharp reproof; upon Geoffrey, however, it had no effect whatsoever.

As for myself, I managed for the most part to keep out of his way, fearful lest he should force me to bathe, or to play French cricket on the lawn. He was obsessed, to an extraordinary degree, by the idea of physical fitness, and there was hardly a moment of the day during which he was not, in one way or another, taking exercise. He was, he announced importantly, "in training", though what he was training for was not specified; I supposed that it had something to do with his ambition to be a soldier, and to kill Germans.

On the last afternoon of the Greenes' visit, I happened to be standing on the balcony outside the dining-room, watching Nigel who, on the lawn below, was amusing himself with the garden hose. He had removed the nozzle, and was playing the single jet, at full cock, across the garden. I guessed that, knowing my family (and his own mother) to be sitting on the terrace below the lawn, screened from above by a thicket of tamarisks, he had conceived the idea of giving them a shower-bath. At that moment I saw Geoffrey—unperceived, however, by Nigel—emerge from the house and cross the lawn.

"Steady on there, with that hose," I heard him say, in his deep, commanding voice.

Nigel turned half towards him, the hose still playing in a high glittering arc across the tamarisks. As I watched, I saw his features take on an expression with which, of late, I had become all too familiar, and which I mentally classified as Nigel's "naughty" face:

a look of compulsive bravado tempered by a helpless awareness of coming disaster.

I saw Geoffrey take a quick step forward; at the same instant Nigel swivelled round and turned the jet of the hose, at point-blank range, full in his brother's face.

The next moment Nigel was lying on the grass, screaming, with the hose, like a long pink snake, entangled between his legs. I saw Geoffrey, streaming with water, dart towards the house and return, an instant later, with a dog-whip in his hand. Hauling Nigel to his feet, he seized him firmly by the shoulders, raising the whip in his right hand; Nigel, however, wriggled like a minnow in his grasp, slewing his head round towards Geoffrey's fingers which clutched the blue serge of his tunic below the neck. Suddenly Geoffrey gave a shout of pain, flung his brother aside, and stood looking down at his left wrist. A moment later, he had recaptured Nigel and, his face distorted by fury, was lashing him violently and repeatedly across the buttocks.

Nigel's screams, however, had not gone unheard, and suddenly I saw my nurse dash out on to the lawn, seize the whip from Geoffrey's hand, and fling it across the garden. Grasping Nigel in her arms, she turned furiously upon Geoffrey who, drenched to the skin, bleeding and utterly dumbfounded by her intervention, was looking, for once in his life, less than dignified.

"I *did* give you more credit," Nurse stormed at him. "You ought to be ashamed of yourself—a big boy like you striking *a child smaller than yourself.*"

Trembling with rage, Geoffrey glared at her with an air of such thunderous menace that for a moment I expected Nurse to be attacked in her turn. What had chiefly rankled, as I could guess, was the implication that, in Nurse's eyes at any rate, he—who would soon be at Sandhurst—could still be classed as a "child".

"B-but look here, Nurse," he spluttered, almost speechless from fury, and looking less self-possessed than I had ever seen him, "d'you realize that the little swine actually *bit* me?"

He held out his bleeding wrist in self-justification. Nurse, however, was unimpressed, and gave him a look which, by rights, should have blasted him on the spot.

"Well, if he did, you've only yourself to blame," she retorted. "And all I can say is, it serves you right. Why, if you were *my* child, I'd have you horse-whipped."

The Greenes departed the next day, much to the relief not only of myself but of the entire household. It was generally agreed that Geoffrey was intolerable, and his brutal assault upon Nigel—retailed in graphic detail by my nurse—did nothing to endear him to my mother, who had always, as she said, thought him "hard" and unsympathetic.

As for my father, he contented himself with looking—at a somewhat steeper angle than usual—down his nose.

It was to be many years before I saw either Nigel or Geoffrey again; nor, with a single exception, did I meet any of the rest of the family—apart from the briefest and most unmemorable of encounters—till I was grown-up. The Greenes, however, continued to be intermittently discussed in my home-circle, and as I grew older my vague childhood impression of the family was replaced by a conception of them more firmly based on facts. I learnt that they were an enormous and ramifying clan who had derived their wealth, in the first instance, from a brewery, Iggulsden and Greene's Entire, with whose inn-signs I was familiar enough in the neighbourhood of our home. Nowadays, the family had no direct connection with the brewery, which had been sold at an enormous profit by old Ebenezer Greene (grandfather of Geoffrey and Nigel), who was something of a financial genius, and had invested his already substantial capital so adroitly that, within less than ten years, he had doubled if not trebled it. Old Ebenezer was a living refutation of the theory that money-making is a sublimation of the sexual instinct, for he had married no less than three times, and produced a total of between twenty and thirty children. About his first wife we knew next to nothing; *en secondes noces*, however, he had married an aunt of my father's, who was responsible for no less than seventeen of his thirty-odd offspring. She died—not surprisingly—at a comparatively early age, and within a year he had married her younger sister, who remained in a permanently interesting condition for the next fifteen years, at the end of which period she too died. The numerous issue of this third marriage were born before the passing of the Deceased Wife's Sister's bill—a trumpery legal point which the old man had airily ignored. When the bill was passed, however, he celebrated the legitimization of his third quiverful by a grand dinner-party at the Savoy Hotel, to which he invited all his surviving relations, including those of his first two wives.

The complex inter-relationships of the Greene family were a fairly frequent topic for conversation at home, supplying my parents—and in later days my brother and sister—with the kind of intellectual exercise which is provided, for persons less genealogically minded, by cross-word puzzles or chess. As for myself, I had no head for this kind of diversion, I thought genealogies tedious, and was convinced moreover, from all I had heard of them, that the Greenes, as a family, were extremely boring. To this day, I find it hard to recollect the exact nature of my own relationship with Nigel and Geoffrey; I think—but I am not sure—that their father, Herbert Greene, was a son of old Ebenezer's marriage to the younger of my two great-aunts.

The only member of the family whom I ever encountered, during my boyhood and early adolescence, was Mrs. Tufnell-Greene, the mother of Geoffrey and Nigel, who did, at infrequent intervals, come to stay with us at Sandgate. The "Tufnell" must, I think, have been a fairly recent addition, and was the source of a good deal of merriment among my family; it was, in fact, Mrs. Greene's maiden name, and her husband had coupled it with his own pre-eminently for snobbish reasons, for Molly Tufnell came of a minor county family, and was distantly related, on her mother's side, to a dull and totally undistinguished Scottish peer. (The Greenes, as a family, tended to practise a prudent if rather unimaginative hypergamy.) My own family could hardly bring themselves to recognize this tiresome piece of ostentation, which was typical, so my mother declared, of the Greenes' innate vulgarity.

Molly Greene was, I suppose, about fifty at the time of which I write, though to me, in my teens, she seemed a good deal older. She was an undistinguished and rather silly woman with the remains of passable good looks, though her grey eyes bulged somewhat too prominently from her long, sallow face: I suspect that she suffered from a mild exophthalmic goitre. She was always extremely well-dressed, in the sense that her hats, her shoes, her coats-and-skirts, etc., came from the best and most expensive shops, yet, inexplicably, she invariably looked dowdy. My mother, who frankly envied her her dress-allowance, would explain this by saying that "poor Molly never knew how to *wear* her clothes". Appearances quite apart, she was a singularly dull person; she didn't read, didn't "care for" music, seldom went to a theatre; her sole interest, apart from her children, seemed to be clothes, which—since she lacked all sense of style—was perhaps a pity. She much enjoyed, too, having long, cosy talks with my mother about the "servant problem" and the running of her enormous house, The Grange, at Blackheath, which could hardly have caused her more mental stress and anxiety if she had possessed no more than a couple of hundred pounds a year instead of (as one guessed) at least ten thousand. With *her* income, my mother was wont to declare, there ought to be no "problems" at all, about servants or anything else.

Molly's children, too, were a constant source of anxiety to her, though there seemed no rational basis for this, since they all—with the possible exception of Nigel—appeared to be perfectly healthy, normal and well-behaved. The eldest, Oonagh, was by now about twenty-eight and still unmarried; she lived at home, but having a passion for horses, had taken a job—at a purely nominal salary, and with a certain amount of opposition from her parents—at a local riding school, which seemed to keep her happily and harmlessly employed. Geoffrey, a year or two younger, had fulfilled, during the latter part of the war, his early ambition to kill Germans; so many had he killed, that he had been awarded the M.C. for it. He was still in the Army at present, but was thinking of sending in his papers—since, as he said, there seemed no likelihood of another "scrap" for the time being—and entering a firm of champagne-shippers, an offshoot of Iggulsden and Greene's Entire, in which his father had an interest. Nigel, who was said to be "difficult", was still at Uppingham.

CHAPTER TWO

The Grange

My father retired from the family business at Folkestone in 1927, and in the late summer of that year we left our house at Sandgate and moved to Blackheath. The Tufnell-Greenes were now our neighbours: their house, The Grange, lay at the opposite end of the Heath from ours, standing in its own large grounds upon the lower slopes of Shooters' Hill. My brother and sister had both visited it before, and described it as being extremely grand though quite indescribably hideous. As for the family themselves, they sounded, from such comments as reached my ears, no less unattractive than the house which they inhabited. Mrs. Greene I knew; her husband, it seemed, was pompous, deaf and could talk of nothing but money; about their children, accounts differed. Geoffrey, according to my brother, was "an ordinary sort of chap", while my sister, more positively, thought him a bounder; Oonagh, by universal consent, was just plain dull. As for Nigel, he seemed to be "a bit of an ass", and was always in trouble: he had been, it appeared, not exactly expelled from Uppingham, but "asked to leave" (nobody quite knew why, though we suspected—at least I did—the worst), and had since been put to work in an insurance office in the City. My mother further reported—on hearsay only, for she had scarcely met him since his childhood—that he was "very artistic", and wanted to take up painting. This item of news did make me prick up my ears: perhaps, I thought, Nigel would turn out to be a romantic, Rimbaud figure, farouche, dirty and iconoclastic; perhaps, on the other hand—for the word "artistic" was susceptible of more than one interpretation—I should be confronted by an exquisite, willowy creature who wore grey suede shoes and quoted the epigrams from *Dorian Gray*.

Another aspect of The Grange which aroused my curiosity was old Mr. Greene's collection of modern French pictures, which were said to be "worth a fortune"; I imagined dazzling vistas of Renoirs, Monets, Matisses, Cézannes, though this scarcely fitted in with my general conception of the Tufnell-Greene ambience. Everything that I had ever heard about them suggested a gross, uncompromising philistinism; could it really be that old Herbert Greene cherished an incongruous passion for the impressionists and the *fauves*? More in keeping, I felt, was Mr. Greene's other and more widely canvassed hobby; he was a horologist of some repute, it seemed, and possessed one of the finest collections of clocks and watches in the south of England. This I found extremely boring, and could hardly believe that so tedious an enthusiasm could be combined with a lively interest in modern art.

I was mildly curious, it is true, about the "artistic" proclivities of Nigel, and about his father's French pictures; yet when we were at last installed in our house in Blackheath Park, the prospect of an imminent visit from the Greenes filled me with mingled boredom and alarm. My vague childhood memories of Geoffrey and Nigel were almost wholly unpleasant and I was convinced that, as a family, the Greenes were—as my mother had once injudiciously confessed—"as dull as ditch-water". Even my father had been heard to remark that they were extremely "conventional"; coming from him, the epithet seemed particularly damning, for he himself could scarcely be described as Bohemian. Myself a born rebel, I was prepared in advance to loathe our cousins, on principle, as it were, and from a sense of duty.

We had not been more than a few days in our new home when the Greenes were invited to tea. A dinner-party had been suggested, but my father had scouted the idea; though possessing a good deal of family loyalty, he really found his cousins insufferably tedious, and was unprepared to perform more than a token-gesture of hospitality. Old Herbert Greene, moreover, had with advancing years become increasingly unsociable, and flatly refused, nowadays, to visit any of his neighbours, even if they were of his own kin. He was represented, therefore, at this tea-party, by Geoffrey who, with his mother and his newly-acquired fiancée, rolled up at four o'clock in a huge and rather old-fashioned Rolls-Royce which, with its black paint-work and highly-polished fittings, resembled some very grand and expensive hearse.

At that age I had a peculiar loathing for such functions, and this one was to exceed my worst expectations. I had hoped that the artistic Nigel would be present, but the day being a weekday, he was at work: "One of the world's workers, you know," as Molly Greene archly expressed it. Oonagh was at work, too, at her riding-school, and Geoffrey himself would normally have been at his office, but had returned, only last night, from a sailing holiday in Devonshire. (The Greenes had a great cult for Work; excessively rich as they were, none of them need ever have done a hand's-turn, but family tradition died hard—the chief use of wealth was to enable its possessor to make still more money.)

Molly was the same as ever—expensively dressed yet dowdy; Geoffrey had grown into an enormous, beefy young man with lowering brows and an expression of imperfectly restrained arrogance. Madge Ullyett, his bride-to-be, was a tall, bony girl with a high, somewhat grating voice. I had gathered that the match was considered, on both sides, to be an eminently satisfactory one; like his father before him, Geoffrey had prudently chosen a wife from a slightly higher social drawer than his own: Madge was the daughter of a retired Colonel of the Buffs, poor but well-connected. Already twenty-eight, and not notably good-looking, she had been fortunate—so it was felt—to secure for herself so rich and so personable a husband.

We sat down to tea; my mother and Molly were soon engrossed in domesticities, Geoffrey talked to my father about the champagne firm in which he was now employed. I found myself chatting, desultorily and with a painful shyness, to Madge. She seemed, on the whole, harmless enough, though her pleasant manners struck me as being a trifle brittle, and I could deduce, now and again, a latent streak of bitchiness, as for instance when she spoke of

Geoffrey's sister Oonagh—so plain and, it seemed, so unmarriage-able—for whom, it was evident, she felt a contempt based upon the crudest kind of sexual snobbery.

Soon we were talking about the latest "shows"—at that date, among suburban or provincial people, an almost obligatory social gambit on such occasions as this—and we agreed in admiring the new star, Jessie Matthews, then appearing in *One Dam Thing After Another* at the London Pavilion.

"I thought it was a ripping show," said Madge.

Having exhausted this interesting but somewhat limited topic, I fell silent, wondering what on earth to talk about next.

"I hear," remarked Madge at last, with an amiable show of interest, "that you're a great reader."

I replied—a trifle coldly, for the phrase jarred on me—that I supposed I was, and a vapid discussion ensued as to the respective merits of Galsworthy and Hugh Walpole, both of whom Madge professed to admire, though I was inclined to suspect, from the terms in which she expressed her admiration, that the books she really liked were of the kind which are classified, in circulating libraries, as "light romances". Striking my blow for culture, I countered with Aldous Huxley, but Madge found his novels "unnecessary".

"Of course. I'm not a bit highbrow," she added, with a complacent little laugh. "You'll think me an awful Philistine, I'm afraid."

To this latter remark, which plainly required the answer no, I was rude enough to make no reply. Madge, however, leaping tactfully into the breach, suddenly leaned forward and said, in a tone wholly different from the light, non-committal accents in which she had so far been speaking:

"Of course, I suppose you've known Geoff for years, haven't you?"

I explained that I had, in fact, only met Geoffrey once before in my life, when I was six years old.

"But I expect you remember him, don't you? Do tell me what he was like when he was young."

I felt suddenly embarrassed.

"Honestly," I muttered, feeling myself beginning to blush, "I scarcely remember him at all. He was ten years older than me—practically grown-up. I really remember Nigel better, though I haven't seen *him* since I was six, either."

"Oh yes, Nigel," she echoed, with a perceptible falling-off of interest. "He's awfully *clever*, isn't he?" She accented the word half-ironically, as though paying lip-service to a quality which, perhaps, she regarded—like the novels of Aldous Huxley—as unnecessary.

"My mother says he's very 'artistic'," I said, putting the word into the audible quotation-marks which I felt it deserved.

"Oh yes, he's frightfully highbrow, I believe. I don't know him awfully well, actually—he rather keeps out of my way. I don't expect I'm intellectual enough for him." Once again Madge gave her complacent little laugh. "Geoff's rather down on him, as it happens—he thinks he's unhealthy, doesn't take enough exercise and all that. In fact, between you and me, I fancy there's not much love lost between those two."

This didn't surprise me in the least, but I made some vague, non-committal reply.

"No, well, you see," Madge continued, "they're such utterly different types, really. I mean, Geoff's mad-keen on games and sport, especially rugger, of course. They thought an awful lot of him at Uppingham—I met someone the other day, a friend of Daddy's, who told me. And his club did awfully well last season—Geoff was frightfully bucked, naturally."

As she spoke, her pale, rather expressionless eyes kindled with a genuine enthusiasm, in striking contrast with that which she had professed for the novels of Hugh Walpole, or even for the dancing of Miss Jessie Matthews. I decided that she must really—though her marriage was in part, no doubt, one of convenience—be genuinely in love with Geoffrey; and while she continued to sing his praises, I glanced covertly at the object of her affection across the tea-table. As a human specimen, he was not lacking in good points; his face, in its coarse-grained, inexpressive way, was rather handsome, his body well-formed and admirably muscular. Though now nearly thirty, he was not, I thought, so very different from the haughty youth of sixteen who had stayed with us at Sandgate: there was the same air of bouncing confidence, the same habitual aggressiveness only partially subdued by good manners; I noticed that he seldom smiled, and that if he did so, it was usually with derision; as he talked, he screwed up his eyes and peered before him with an exaggerated intensity which suggested either some innate difficulty in concentrating or—more probably—a neglected tendency to astigmatism.

My father now came over to talk to Madge, and, exchanging my chair for his, I found myself condemned, inescapably, to a *tête-à-tête* with Geoffrey. I was frankly terrified, knowing him to be the sort of person with whom I was least in sympathy; at the same time, I was humiliatingly aware of a perverse desire—surviving, perhaps, from those far-off days at Sandgate—to impress him favourably. He might be a brainless lout, but I knew, in my heart, that I envied him for being all that I was not: self-confident, extroverted, physically tough.

I sat down gingerly in the chair by his side: painfully aware of my awkwardness, my spindly, unathletic body and the eruption of adolescent pimples upon my chin. My clothes, too, were hopelessly wrong: silver-grey Oxford bags, a double-breasted brown coat (too tight in the waist), a soft collar and—worst of all—an orange shantung tie. Geoffrey, I was convinced, must have already concluded that I was not only decadent but downright depraved: a waster, a long-haired artist (nervously I raised my hand to the nape of my neck—I hadn't had a haircut for a month), probably a sodomite. Geoffrey himself wore a dark suit, a stiff collar and an old Uppinghamian tie. As I sat down, he gave me a brief, disdainful glance from beneath his bushy eyebrows, rather as though I were a boy from the lower-fourth who had been summoned for an interview with the head of the house. What on earth, I wondered desperately, should I find to talk about to this bouncing, art-hating rugger player?

As it happened, I need not have worried, for Geoffrey appeared only too willing—and indeed anxious—to do all the talking himself.

"D'you sail?" he shot at me abruptly.

"Do I what?" I queried, flustered by his manner into a temporary deafness.

"Done any sailing—small boat sailing, I mean? Jolly fine sport, you ought to take it up. Fact is, I'm just back from a spell of it, down in Devon—chap I know has a boat down there, on the Torridge, and asked me to make up his crew . . ."

It was as though a gramophone or wireless-set had suddenly been turned on: in his brusque, telegraphic style, shooting out his words like a drill-sergeant, Geoffrey proceeded forthwith to lecture me, at enormous length and with an immense wealth of technical detail, about his sailing adventures in Devon. The fact that I was a complete ignoramus and made no attempt to conceal it didn't worry him in the least: all that he needed was an audience, preferably a silent one. For a good ten minutes the harsh, grating voice went booming mercilessly on: my head buzzed with the unfamiliar nautical jargon—jibs, booms, spinnakers and the rest. I had never felt so bored in my life; at last—just as I was beginning to feel that I couldn't bear it a moment longer—I saw him glance at his watch. He gave a sharp exclamation, and instantly the spate of his talk was switched off, as abruptly as it had begun. He jumped from his chair and, crossing to the sofa where his mother was sitting, announced—in an unnecessarily loud voice, as though Molly were deaf—that it was time to go. The rugger club for which he played had a practice game that evening, and he had promised to show up.

"It's later than I thought," he exclaimed, with ill-concealed impatience. "I take it you're going straight home, Mother? We can drop you on the way."

Mrs. Greene, however, was not going straight home: she had promised to pay a visit to an old family servant living at Catford, which lay in the opposite direction, and she was already late. A silly and (on Geoffrey's side) rather an ill-tempered argument ensued. Suggestions and counter-suggestions flew back and forth: Molly, displaying an unusual obstinacy, was reluctant to let down "poor old Nelly"; Geoffrey, for his part, was grimly determined to be up at the football ground by six o'clock. Our own car, by a stroke of ill-luck, was under repair at the garage; it was already a quarter to six, and Molly had promised to be at Catford by half-past five, but if the car took her there first, Geoffrey would be late for his game. Things seemed at a deadlock: Molly was flustered and near to tears, and I could see that Geoffrey's temper was rising.

"Oh all right," he burst out at last, with an air of tragic self-sacrifice, "I'd better give up my game."

It was at this moment that Madge was impelled, not very happily, to intervene with the suggestion that she and Geoffrey should go up to the ground by bus.

Her lover threw her a contemptuous glance.

"You know perfectly well it can't be done," he snapped. "It'd take us a good half-hour by the time we'd picked up a bus in the village."

"Oh, all right, sorry I spoke," Madge replied, with jaunty sarcasm, her voice trailing off into a shrill, nervous titter.

At this Geoffrey, who had been inwardly fuming with rage for the past few minutes, finally lost his temper.

"I fail to see what there is to laugh at," he bawled at her insolently.

I saw poor Madge go white. There was a moment's horrified silence, tense and overcharged as the stillness which follows a thunderclap. I glanced from Geoffrey to Madge, from Madge to Mrs. Greene: appalled yet fascinated by the spectacle of these three staid, conventional people tottering upon the brink of the social abyss.

Then, like the sudden rush of air into a vacuum, everybody started to talk at once. I heard my mother ask Geoffrey to ring for the parlourmaid, Mrs. Greene uttered some lenitive observation about the weather, Madge gushed over the cat who, with notable tact, had chosen that moment to sidle in from the garden. Geoffrey, with a parade-ground smartness, leapt to obey my mother's command, his face once more a blank, inexpressive mask.

My father, with a sudden and belated inspiration, suggested ordering a taxi to take Geoffrey and Madge up to the ground.

Geoffrey greeted this with an exaggerated outburst of enthusiasm, obviously regretting that he hadn't thought of it himself.

"Buck up, my girl," he shouted at Madge. "I'll go and 'phone for the taxi while you're getting your traps together. I've got my rugger kit in the Rolls, by the way—you might see it's taken out before Mother goes."

Madge, who was inclined to parsimony, protested that to take a taxi would be "wickedly extravagant".

"I'm not asking you to pay for it, am I?" Geoffrey snapped at her.

Our guests departed at last: Geoffrey and Madge in the taxi (Madge looking taut and resentful), Mrs. Greene in the funereal Rolls, driven by Thornton, the smart but suitably gloomy chauffeur. Molly still looked flustered and inclined to tears, and I felt rather sorry for her; as for Geoffrey, I thought him a brute and a boor, and I decided, there and then, that I would have no more to do with him.

The Greenes, however, now that they were our neighbours, were not so easily avoided, and only a week after that uncomfortable tea-party we were invited, in our turn, to tea with them. My father, as it happened, had a prior engagement, and it fell to me to escort my mother to The Grange on the following Sunday.

We drove across the Heath in our humble Minerva. The car, by our own modest standards, had up till now seemed to me rather a grand one; beside the Greenes' Rolls, however, I was aware that it must seem a very second-rate affair, and I wondered why I should mind. To offset the inferiority of the car—and of our chauffeur-gardener, who was not to be compared with the immaculate Thornton—I had prudently assumed a dark suit and a soberly patterned tie of which even Geoffrey, I felt, could scarcely disapprove.

At last we reached The Grange: a wrought-iron gateway led through a high brick wall into a curving drive, flanked by dingy laurels and Wellingtonias. I had heard much about the hideousness of the Greenes' house, and had indeed formed a vague mental picture of Gothic horrors in store; but I was totally unprepared for the Nightmare Abbey which, as we turned a corner of the drive, burst upon my view.

Built by old Ebenezer Greene in, I suppose, about 1870, the enormous mansion was a fitting monument to the wealth, the fertility and the aggressive philistinism of its founder. The brickwork was of that peculiarly institutional shade of greyish-yellow which one associates with Victorian gaols and public lavatories, inset below the cornices with small, rectangular red and blue tiles. The façade was of a relatively sober design, predominantly Venetian Gothic with a felicitous suggestion, here and there, of late Jacobean; it was in the upper storeys, however, that the architect had allowed his ebullient fancy its fullest play, and at roof-level the house blossomed into a perfect riot of machicolations, pinnacles, otiose gables, buttresses and Gothic turrets. This note of fantasy was repeated in the stables, vaguely ecclesiastical in feeling, with a spiky little clock tower, which lay slightly to the rear of the building; on the opposite side, in sight of the front door, projected a vast domed conservatory, like a miniature version of the Crystal Palace.

It was a grey, lowering afternoon in late September, and the house, set among thickets of conifers, exhaled an air of dank, sabbatical gloom; nor was this impression contradicted when, having rung the massive, brass-handled bell (of that primitive kind which communicates, by a system of jangling wires, with the servants' quarters), we were admitted by the butler, a taciturn man whom my mother, familiar with the household, addressed as Graves. The hall, vast and baronial, struck a chill: with its bogus fan-vaulting and perspectives of Gothic arches, it suggested, more than anything else, the setting for a mid-Victorian production of *Lucia di Lammermoor*. This unpleasing effect was enhanced by two stained-glass lancet windows, the livid and inflamed colouring of which reminded me of the illustrations, in a medical dictionary, of the more disgusting kinds of skin-disease.

The drawing-room, as Graves ushered us into it, seemed to be crowded with people; as my vision adjusted itself to the scene, I saw that in fact only five persons were present besides ourselves:

Molly Greene, a bald-headed old gentleman who must be her husband, Madge Ullyett and two others—neither of whom, I observed with relief, was Geoffrey. My phantasmagoric impression had been due—as I realized a moment later—to the vast quantities of furniture which, lining the walls, projecting at awkward angles, and disposed obstructively over every available yard of floor-space, left only a small central area, in front of the fireplace, for the accommodation of the room's occupants.

Here Mrs. Greene sat enthroned before the tea-table, the space about her further encumbered by an astonishing collection of bags, without which she seemed incapable of stirring even from one end of the room to the other. What they contained I never knew, though various oddments of half-darned socks, balls of wool, newspapers and so forth could be seen to protrude from their orifices. There were bags and baskets of every description: Italian bags of plaited straw, Swiss baskets with lids, leather bags, silk bags, string bags and even, I seem to remember, a small garden trug. Her husband stood with his back to the hearth where—though it was only September, and the weather mild—a huge fire blazed.

Herbert Greene, to whom I was now introduced, was one of the most physically repellent men I have ever met: grossly fat, with an enormous paunch, he had almost no neck, his head appearing to sprout directly from between his shoulders. He was almost totally bald, and his scalp was mottled with confluent brownish patches, as though infested with some fungus or lichen. The face beneath, coarse-grained and of an apoplectic crimson, was pear-shaped, with a heavy, underhung jowl; his lips were loose and fleshy, and he was inclined to spit as he talked. He was also very deaf, but would not admit the fact, and refused to have an ear-trumpet; if one shouted at him he became annoyed, if one spoke in ordinary tones he would order one, sharply, to speak up. His voice was harsh and rather husky, with traces of a slight, ineradicable Cockney accent.

He greeted me perfunctorily, then turned aside to speak to my mother. I exchanged a word or two with Madge (who was staying for the week-end), then became aware that the two other members of the party were waiting to be introduced to me. One of these was Oonagh: an inconspicuous young woman with mousy, shingled hair, horn-rimmed spectacles and spots. The other was a tall bony young man of about my own age, also with spots; like Oonagh, he wore spectacles, but as he came forward to greet me, he took them off, and peered at me, short-sightedly, with an air of detached and rather supercilious curiosity.

"You remember Nigel, don't you?" said Molly. "I'm sure you'll have lots to talk about, you used to be such friends in the old days, didn't you?"

We glared at one another mistrustfully, tacitly disclaiming this imputed bond of fellowship.

"Such a pity Geoffrey couldn't be here, he's playing golf down at Walton Heath," Molly added.

I found myself at last seated between Nigel and Oonagh, engaged in the most vapid of small talk. So this, I thought, was the famous Nigel: a perfectly ordinary, rather ugly young man, dressed unexceptionably in a tweed suit and a Paisley-patterned tie. Not by any stretch of imagination could he be allotted to either of the two rôles for which, in anticipation, I had cast him: he was neither willowy nor particularly farouche, there was nothing about him either of Rimbaud or of Wilde. I was badly disappointed; but perhaps, I thought hopefully—since I had been so repeatedly assured that he was artistic—he subscribed to the modern view that poets should look like bankers or stockbrokers. Eliot, after all, had worked in a bank, and looked like it; Nigel was in an insurance office, and might well be writing a new *Waste Land* in his spare time.

If such, however, were really the case, he was certainly (I thought) an adept at concealing his secret proclivities. From the new Cochran revue, the conversation turned to Noel Coward, and thence to Michael Arlen. Once again—as with Madge on a previous occasion—I extolled the merits of Aldous Huxley.

"Aldous Huxley?" said Nigel. "Oh yes, didn't he write something called *Crazy Pavements*? Rather amusing in its way—a bit *risqué*, too."

So Nigel, I decided regretfully, was not a highbrow after all.

As for poor Oonagh—she was invariably referred to as "poor", even by her own family—she was really a pathetically dim person; nor did she make any but the most half-hearted efforts to compensate for her natural disadvantages. She was dressed, today, in an unbecoming green dress, with a demure and unfashionable V-neck; her face was innocent of make-up (no unusual omission, for girls like Oonagh, in 1927), and her hair looked as though it could do with a good wash. Having so far taken almost no part in the conversation, she now launched herself into a detailed and excessively tedious description of a holiday in Scotland, which she facetiously referred to as the Land of Cakes. I made no attempt to interrupt her monologue, though Nigel interpolated an occasional derisory or critical remark. Looking at him, I decided that he had changed remarkably little since his childhood. Now, as then, his face wore a permanent expression of resentment; this may have been partly due to his myopia—I noticed that, from vanity, he wore his spectacles as little as possible (my nurse had doubtless been right in suspecting that his childish outbursts of temper had had something to do with bad eyesight). Now that his voice had broken, he spoke with a curiously unnatural, plummy accent, altogether too gentlemanly to be true; he sounded like an amateur actor attempting some unsympathetic and incongruous part upon the stage.

While Oonagh continued to praise the Land of Cakes, I had leisure to examine my surroundings. I had often heard my parents speak of the drawing-room at The Grange: old Herbert, it was said, had collected some wonderful "pieces", and must have spent a fortune on them. This—though I was, and still am, extremely ignorant about antiques—I found quite easy to believe: the Sheraton and Chippendale were, I had no doubt, of the very best and most authentic; so were the Chinese lacquer cabinets, the cupboards full of glass and porcelain, the marquetry tables and all the rest. But they were so overcrowded, and jumbled in such inextricable confusion, that their effect was nullified. There was, for that matter, a good deal of rubbish, perhaps representing Molly's—rather than her husband's—taste: rows of indifferent water-colours in wide gilt mounts; mahogany pedestals with bowls from which depended etiolated swathes of smilax; whatnots loaded with small and hideous objects, pouffes covered with silk tassels and garish embroidery. To all this, the wallpaper supplied a singularly inappropriate and distracting background: patterned with black vertical stripes, with swags of pink rambler roses, it was of the kind which I could just remember as having been fashionable in about 1916; the curtains, the chair-covers and the elaborate fringed lampshades gave a similar impression of self-conscious but, by now, outdated *chic*. The whole room, in fact, protested too much, and in too many different tones of voice. Even the cat seemed overdressed: a big, long-haired ginger tom (though gelded, of course), he looked for all the world as though he had been dressed up in his mistress's fox-furs especially for the occasion.

Meanwhile I was eating an enormous tea. The Greenes never did anything by halves, and the apparatus of tea at The Grange had the same quality of excess which pervaded the entire household. The food provided on this occasion would have more than satisfied a busload of hungry schoolboys; the tea-table was covered with plates of sandwiches and cakes, a curate's joy offered other and even more succulent alternatives, the fireplace was crowded with muffineers containing tea-cake, scones and anchovy toast. Presently chairs were shifted and a kind of general post occurred, at the end of which I found myself sitting next to my host. This seemed a good moment to satisfy my curiosity about the French pictures, and I asked politely whether I might see them.

"Speak up, boy, speak up!" grumbled Mr. Greene, peevishly.

I repeated my request, in a voice rendered excessively loud by my nervousness.

"All right, all right, don't shout at me, I'm not deaf . . . Pictures, eh? Interested in pictures, are you? Quite a nice little collection I've got—French stuff, mostly. Modern, you know—can't afford Watteau and Greuze, and those fellows. Got a nice Corot, though: gave a pretty stiff price for it, too, but it's worth it, I'm told—Corots are going up."

"Have you", I asked, adjusting my voice to what I hoped was the right pitch, "any Monets?"

"Eh, what's that? Speak up, can't you, me boy?"

I repeated my question.

The swollen, batrachian face suddenly assumed a darker tinge, the deeply-embedded eyes glared at me ferociously.

"What's that you say, me boy—have I got any *money*?"

"Not money, *Monet*," I shouted.

Mr. Greene continued to stare at me with outraged incomprehension: perhaps he supposed that I was trying to touch him for a fiver.

"Monet!" I bawled again, "the painter—one of the Impressionists."

"Oh, you mean *Mohnay*," he said at last, disdainfully. "Naow, naow, I don't go in for those futurist fellows." He heaved himself from his chair. "Come along with me, me boy—I'll show you some really decent stuff. Used to be quite a hobby of mine—more interested in clocks, nowadays . . . Fellow at the club, an R.A., put me on to the right things to go for. Some time ago now, but that chap knew what he was talking about."

By this time I had followed the old man out into the hall, but he was in no hurry to show me the famous pictures. As we proceeded along the passage towards the room, at the back of the house, where they were hung, Mr. Greene paused at least half-a-dozen times to point out to me one or another of the innumerable clocks which projected from the walls. Of every conceivable date and style, they struck me as being uniformly and defiantly hideous; I daresay I was wrong, but I was totally ignorant of the science (or art) of horology, the name of Tompion meant nothing to me, and I found Mr. Greene's disquisitions excruciatingly boring. Once mounted, however, upon his hobby-horse, he could not easily be dislodged, and it must have been quite twenty minutes before he opened a door at the end of the passage and led me into a long room which, lighted only by narrow windows inset with the same garish and repellent glass as those in the hall, was so dark that its contents were almost wholly invisible.

"Used to be the billiard-room," my host explained, "but it didn't answer—not enough elbow-room, you know. I did build out another one, at the back, but it's hardly been used—Geoff's not keen, and if I want a game I can get it at the club."

It was typical of the Greenes' exorbitant way of life, I thought, to build enormous billiard-rooms which were never used. At this moment the old man switched on a battery of lights, the room leapt into sudden brilliance, and the pictures were revealed.

I had guessed that I was in for a disappointment, and hardly expected, at this stage, to be greeted by the Manets and Sisleys, the sumptuous Renoirs and glittering Seurats of my earlier imagining; nonetheless I was stupefied, as my eyes accustomed themselves to the sudden blaze of light, by the spectacle before me. There must have been over a hundred pictures, in heavy and over-ornate gilt frames, crowded in three rows upon the walls; but in place of the fresh, vivid colours, the shimmering light-effects with which the conjoined words "modern" and "French" were, for me, indissolubly associated, I was confronted with canvas after canvas painted in dull and curiously greasy-looking tones which reminded me of nothing so much as the oleographs so proudly displayed in the parlours of seaside boarding-houses. It was a far cry indeed from my conception of what was meant by modern French painting; I had been to the Tate and even to the Luxembourg, I had read my Roger Fry and my Clive Bell, but such names as Bouguereau, Henner, Bastien-Lepage, Delaroche or Meissonier were virtually unknown to me—or, if known, remembered only as the targets for some malicious gibe on the part of Mr. Bell or Mr. Fry, who would doubtless have dismissed Mr. Greene's collection, in its entirety, as "salon art" of the most ignoble kind.

Bouguereau seemed a particular favourite with the old man: stationing himself before a large canvas depicting a female nude, of a peculiarly unpleasant fish-belly whiteness, posed against a background of dark blue rocks, he expatiated freely upon its merits.

"That chap Bouguereau" (he pronounced the name with an appalling mutilation of the vowel-sounds, so that it sounded like "Buggeroo"), "he was a Master of Line. He's been compared to Ingres, you know. And look at those flesh-tints"—he pointed to the lady's tummy, which was painted in tones suggesting the phosphorescent pallor of a decaying bloater—"and those shadows in the background . . . Yes, he was a great painter, was Buggeroo—a Modern Master, you might say."

There were a lot of Bouguereaus and a lot of Henners, each of which demanded an appropriate comment from its proud possessor. Here and there I noticed a picture which I recognized as being, even by Bloomsbury standards, comparatively respectable: a pleasing Millet, a Harpignies, a Théodore Rousseau; there was also the famous Corot—a characteristic landscape of tall, pollarded trees. But Mr. Greene was not much interested in landscape; what he really liked, as he freely confessed, was the human figure—by which, of course, he meant the female figure, in a state of partial or complete undress. Nudes, indeed, predominated; one and all were painted in that peculiarly lubricious yet drearily lifeless style at which French salon painters excel. Mr. Greene's tastes were, in fact, quite simply pornographic, but the smut, to be acceptable, had to be tactfully disguised beneath a veneer of Art, and respectable art at that—as exhibited at the Paris Salon, and vouched for by an R.A. who belonged to the Carlton Club or the Bath. The R.A., I thought, must have gauged Mr. Greene's propensities to a nicety, and advised him accordingly. (I was to learn afterwards that, in the more rigidly conventional circles of Blackheath society, the old man was considered, on account of his collection, to be rather a dashing character—even, perhaps, a bit of a Bohemian; my elderly aunts, confronted by so many—and such very naked-looking— nudes, were certainly of this opinion. It was tacitly conceded, however, that this doggish streak could be easily condoned in so rich and, in all other respects, so worthy a figure as Herbert Greene.)

The tour of the gallery being at last concluded, Mr. Greene proposed a visit to the greenhouses.

"Yer mother tells me you're interested in flowers," he remarked. With some reluctance I admitted that I was, and rather limply followed him along the corridor and out of a side-door into the immense conservatory. It was true that I was by way of being an amateur botanist, but my interest in plants was confined, for the most part, to the indigenous British flora, and certainly didn't extend to the kind of flowers favoured by Mr. Greene. Sweating uncomfortably in the damp heat, I plodded round in his wake, while he extolled the beauties of one hybrid monstrosity after another. His taste in flowers, like his taste in pictures, might fairly have been described as pornographic: never have I seen such obscenely mottled begonias, or calceolarias so shamelessly tumescent; as for the orchids, no nice girl, one felt, would have cared to wear them in her corsage. The gardener at The Grange, one could guess—like Mr. Greene's R.A. friend—was well aware of his master's tastes, and dutifully pandered to them.

As we wandered round the greenhouse, Mr. Greene bumbling his encomiums upon these floral equivalents of Bouguereau and Gustave Moreau, I found myself observing him with the somewhat reluctant attention which I accorded to the plants themselves. There was, I thought, about the Greenes, a quality ineradicably plebeian; obtrusively evident in the old man, it could be discerned, in a modified form, in Geoffrey, in Nigel and even in the dim, unemphatic personality of Oonagh. The Greenes, I suppose, had been technically "gentlefolk" for at least three or four generations—in the restricted sense of being rich enough to send their children to public schools and universities; yet no amount of education or upper-class conditioning seemed able to efface that racial strain of coarseness, betraying itself in the thickened, almost porcine texture of the skin, in the bone-structure of their faces, even in the way the hair sprouted from their heads. For as long as I could remember, I had heard the Greenes referred to as common, and in later years, influenced by the vague and uncommitted leftiness instilled at Bedales, had been wont to deprecate what seemed to me snobbishness on the part of my parents. Yet I now felt compelled to admit that their judgment had been amply justified. If the word meant anything at all, the Greenes *were* common, in the most basic and unequivocal sense. Their commonness had nothing to do with class-shibboleths, they didn't say "Pardon?" or call their napkins serviettes; they were, quite simply, common in being—both in physique and character—irremediably coarse-grained, oafish and lacking in all capacity for subtlety or finesse.

In most families who have climbed from the proletariat or the small-trader class into the high bourgeoisie, the hereditary type is rapidly modified, the plebeian roughness is overlaid with a veneer of good manners and acquired prejudices, till at last, in the space of two or three generations—often less—the end-product is barely distinguishable, both physically and in his psychological make-up, from the most pukka of pukka sahibs. Not so, however, with the Greenes; they remained, for all their wealth and grandeur, as crudely plebeian as old Joseph Greene, the son of a farrier and grandfather of Ebenezer, who had started the family brewery. Not even their habit of marrying—as old Herbert had done, and Geoffrey was about to do—into a higher social class than their own, could succeed in diluting their biological inheritance; in the Greene family the male genes remained firmly and irrepressibly in the ascendant.

At last we returned to the drawing-room. Here it was suggested, by Molly, that Nigel should show me round the garden; this he agreed, without much enthusiasm, to do, and Madge, for some reason, decided to accompany us.

We trailed out, rather drearily, on to the lawn. The afternoon was still overcast and gloomy, it had rained heavily in the morning, and the garden was dripping with a steamy and soot-laden moisture.

"There's really nothing to see," Nigel remarked resentfully. "Rodgers has got some prize marrows down in the kitchen garden, but they're really just like other marrows, only bigger and more horrible."

"You're so lucky to be able to grow rhododendrons," Madge commented brightly, pointing to a clump of funereal and grimy foliage. "*We* can't make them do, but of course we're on chalk."

A lawn swept down from the house to the tennis courts, beyond which, decently screened by a hedge of euonymus, lay the kitchen garden; in front of the house a series of flower-beds—circular, lozenge or star shaped—displayed geometrically disposed patterns of geranium, lobelia and scarlet salvia. In the herbaceous border, flanking the high garden wall, Michaelmas daisies smouldered dimly in the grey, brackish light; lower down, near the tennis courts, stood a group of apple trees, and beneath them a scatter of windfalls lay rotting in the wet grass.

"It's time Rodgers picked *those* up," remarked Madge. "They'll only be wasted if he doesn't."

"Good Lord, *they're* no good," Nigel retorted contemptuously. "We've got masses of apples in the orchard, round the other side. We never bother to gather these—they're frightfully sour, you can hardly use them for cooking even."

"But d'you mean to say they'll just be left there to *rot*?" Madge exclaimed, in shocked tones.

"Why ever not?" Nigel snapped impatiently. "Rodgers'll probably use them for manure—that's all they're fit for, anyway."

"Well, if that's the case, I'm going to take some home," Madge declared. "I can't *stand* waste."

Without another word, she began to pick up the rotting fruit and stuff it into her bag. We watched her for a few moments as she stooped purposefully to her task; then Nigel moved away towards the tennis courts, and I followed him.

"My God, that girl's mean," he muttered, when we were out of earshot. "She'd go and scrabble in the dustbins, if she thought nobody was looking. I'm sorry for Geoff, I must say—I shouldn't think he'd ever get a decent square meal, when he's married."

Nigel gave a sudden burst of laughter: a shrill, neighing cachinnation which struck me as being somehow out of character.

"By the way," he shot at me, "what did you think of the pater?"

I blushed, as much for his sake as my own: one simply didn't ask such questions of an almost total stranger. I mumbled some vague remark to the effect that I scarcely knew Mr. Greene.

Nigel looked irritatingly self-possessed.

"Oh, all right, you needn't bother to be polite," he said. "I expect the old boy enjoyed showing you all his lovely nudes: pretty hot stuff, some of them—at least, *he* thinks so. Actually, he knows next to nothing about Art—it's good old Sex that *he's* after."

"You're a painter yourself, aren't you?" I asked, tactfully changing the subject, which I found embarrassing.

"Oh, I do a little," Nigel admitted, with another shrill little spurt of laughter. "I'm frightfully bad, actually. The point is, I don't get enough time to really settle down to anything—not while I'm stuck in this bloody job. What I want is to go to an art school and study properly."

"Couldn't you do that?" I asked sympathetically.

"Not on your life," Nigel snorted. "The pater's dead against it, and Geoff backs him up. Everything Geoff says goes, of course—the pater thinks he can do no wrong. You see," he finished, in a smugly complacent tone, "I've always been the family black sheep. Well, I mean to say, wouldn't *you* be if you had Geoff for an elder brother?"

"It's a shame you shouldn't be allowed to do what you want to do," I said, feeling a renewed gust of sympathy, though I still found Nigel's attitude to his family regrettable.

"Oh well," Nigel said, with a histrionic shrug, "one doesn't really expect people like the pater and Geoff to understand."

He had paused in his stride, and stood glaring at me with a taut, nervous defiance; just so, I remembered, had he been accustomed to glare at my nurse, years ago, after some violent outburst of naughtiness.

"D'you remember", I said suddenly, "when you came to stay with us at Sandgate? I must have been about six at the time, and you were a year or so older."

Nigel stared at me vaguely.

"Yes, I do remember we came down . . . You had a canoe, didn't you? Geoff was there too—he had a row with your nurse, or something."

"You turned the hose in his face, and he beat you, and then my nurse went for him."

"Oh, yes, I remember that—I bit Geoff's hand, and he was livid."

"We all thought you were terribly naughty," I said.

Nigel gave a complacent little smirk.

"I daresay I was—Geoff was enough to make anyone kick over the traces. He still is, for that matter."

We had wandered round the tennis courts, by now, and were

standing at the corner of the kitchen garden. A sudden little flicker of friendliness, evoked by our shared memories, had sprung up between us.

"I'd like to see some of your paintings, sometime," I said.

"Oh, all right," Nigel said, looking bored. "I'm not really a bit good." He gave a deep sigh. "To tell you the truth," he added, "I'm really more interested in music, at the moment."

"D'you mean *composing* music?" I said, impressed in spite of myself.

"Well, I've written one or two pieces," he confessed, modestly.

"I'd love to hear them," I said. It might be, I thought, that I had misjudged Nigel: perhaps, after all, he was a great artist—painter, composer and (for all I knew) poet as well, a genius on the grand scale, like some figure of the Renaissance; though, to tell the truth, I didn't—glancing sideways at his dull, rather stupid face, so obviously the face of a Greene—think this very likely.

"D'you know Stravinsky's *Sacre du Printemps*?" he asked me suddenly.

I said I did, and he proceeded to rave about it with what seemed to me—though I quite liked the ballet—a disproportionate enthusiasm. From the *Sacre* he passed to *Petrouchka*, of which he also approved. He mentioned several other works—most of them, I noticed, extremely tumultuous and noisy. My own tastes in music were rather quieter, and I proffered the names of Debussy, Ravel and Delius. Of the last he had not even heard; Ravel he thought "dull", and as for Debussy, the sole work of his with which he seemed to be acquainted was *L'Après-midi d'un Faune*. To this he extended a qualified approval.

"It's so frightfully *sensual*, isn't it?" he said.

I replied that I supposed it was, though it was not this aspect of the work which had chiefly impressed me.

"Have you seen the ballet?" he asked (he pronounced it, very preciously, as "bah-lay").

I had not; my acquaintance with the ballet was limited to a single matinée during the Diaghileff season a year or so previously, and this had not included the Faun. Nigel, however, seemed to

47

have seen a great many ballets, and his knowledgeable chatter made me feel rather dim and provincial.

"I think the bah-lay's absolutely *marvellous*," he exclaimed, in his oddly pitched, plummy voice.

Just then Madge caught up with us, her bag bulging with windfalls, and we strolled back towards the house. To my relief, my mother was already standing by the front door, preparing to leave. Our departure was slightly delayed, however, by the irruption of Geoffrey, back from his golf at Walton Heath.

In a suit of rather loud and very baggy plus-fours, he looked more aggressive and overbearing than ever; he greeted my mother and myself with his usual perfunctory good manners, then turned sharply towards Nigel.

"Did you remember to take in those nets from the tennis courts, as I told you?" he snapped.

I saw Nigel's air of jaunty self-possession suddenly crumple: he looked guilty, subservient and rather frightened.

"I'm sorry, Geoff, I clean forgot," he apologized, in a flat spiritless voice very different from the defiant tones in which, a few minutes ago, he had been speaking of Geoffrey and his father.

"Well, for God's sake go and do it now, and look sharp about it," Geoffrey barked. I saw Nigel slink away, without another word, sullen, mutely resentful and looking not in the least like a many-talented genius of the Renaissance.

We escaped at last: Geoffrey, with brusque politeness, helped my mother into the car; to myself he hardly uttered a word. Perhaps, I thought, he had never really forgiven me for being sick over his best trousers and his coloured socks in the cab from Shorncliffe, on that hot summer's day in 1914. As he leaned forward to say good-bye, his breath smelt slightly of whisky, and my mother noticed it.

"I do hope," she said, as we drove off, "that Geoffrey doesn't *drink*."

CHAPTER THREE

The Fortunes of Nigel

I went up to Oxford that autumn, and during the year which I spent—or, more accurately, misspent—at the University, I saw little of the Tufnell-Greenes, save for an occasional tea or luncheon party. These functions could have given little pleasure to the Greenes (with the possible exception of Molly, who was genuinely fond of my mother), and certainly gave even less to my own family; the ties of kinship, however, must be preserved, and at intervals of a month or so invitations would duly be exchanged.

Whenever possible, I kept out of the way on these occasions. I found the Greenes both boring and boorish, and even my mild curiosity about Nigel's activities as painter and composer had been all but forgotten in the excitement of making new friends at Oxford, many of whom could well have been described, by Mrs. Greene or my own mother, as artistic—some of them, indeed, might have warranted a stronger epithet. By comparison, Nigel seemed to be gauche and unfledged: during this period I hardly ever saw him alone; once or twice I did ask him about his painting or his music, but more from politeness than from any very lively interest. He didn't, however, seem particularly anxious to discuss the subject; he made no offer to show me his pictures or to play me his compositions, so that at last I ceased to enquire about them. He was still working at his insurance office, though he continued, at intervals, to outrage his parents by demanding that he should be allowed to attend an art school—failing which, he would run away to sea, enlist in the Army, or in some other unspecified way disgrace the name of Greene.

A luncheon at The Grange—it must have been during the

Christmas vacation, for I remember that we ate turkey and plum-pudding—remains in my memory by reason of a small incident which struck me as throwing a new and rather sinister light upon the family life of the Greenes. This lunch was by way of being a belated celebration, for the benefit of various members of the family who had not attended the function itself, of Geoffrey's marriage to Madge. They had been married, with much pomp, early in December, and after a honeymoon in Switzerland were now settled in a house on the downs above Wrotham. There were present at lunch, besides the immediate family, representatives of the Richard Greenes, the Walter Greenes and several other of the innumerable offshoots of the clan; one and all, they exhibited that same coarse-grained, plebeian appearance that I had noticed in Herbert Greene and his children. The luncheon was enormous and elaborate, extremely well-cooked and served with a great deal of ceremony. Food at the Greenes was always excellent; plain English cooking, for the most part, but the very best of its kind. Their beef came from Scotland, their turkeys from Norfolk, kippers for breakfast were sent from Whitby (Molly had a standing order); vegetables were all home-grown and of admirable quality, though their excellence was sometimes impaired by a tendency to gigantism, due to the gardener's incurable passion for winning prizes at local flower shows (never have I eaten such outsize asparagus as at The Grange, nor such enormous peas). The wine, too, was first-rate (the Greenes were good customers of my father, who was a wine-merchant), though too often one was compelled to drink champagne throughout the meal, despite the fact that Herbert Greene rather prided himself upon his taste in claret.

Today, of course, being an occasion for celebration, there was champagne. I was sitting opposite Geoffrey, and I noticed that he drank a good deal; Madge, placed between him and his father, looked slightly disapproving, and herself refused wine, after her first glass, with an emphasis which was intended, no doubt, to convey a hint. Towards the end of lunch, Geoffrey, who had lately bought a new and very up-to-date motor-car, and seemed—characteristically enough—unable to talk about anything but his new toy, related a somewhat involved anecdote about a bill for repairs from his local garage. The garage, it seemed, had by some clerical error undercharged, by a quite substantial amount, for the work done. Geoffrey had duly paid the bill, without questioning the total: perhaps he hadn't even noticed the mistake, though this seemed hardly probable, for he had doubtless had an estimate, and was in any case habitually careful about money.

"And then, the other day," he continued, with a derisory chuckle, "they had the cheek to send me in a bill for the balance, with a cringing letter of apology for their own carelessness. Naturally, I've taken no notice—I hope it teaches them a lesson, that's all I can say. I can't stand inefficiency."

Old Mr. Greene had apparently not caught the last sentence or two, for he leaned forward with a puzzled frown.

"What's that, me boy? Sent the bill in again, did they?"

Geoffrey repeated the latter part of the story with a rather unnecessary loudness.

"I've taken no notice, and I don't intend to," he concluded, with a contemptuous laugh.

I saw Mr. Greene's frown deepen, and his eyes were suddenly stern.

"D'you mean to say you'll refuse to pay the balance?" he said gruffly.

"If they're fools enough to undercharge me, that's their lookout," Geoffrey replied jauntily, but I could see that he was not quite at his ease. "If people are inefficient, they deserve to lose by it," he added, in an arrogantly self-righteous tone which didn't, however, quite carry conviction.

Mr. Greene cleared his throat sharply, glanced down at his plate, and muttered, rather testily:

"Of course you must pay up, me boy—of course you must."

Geoffrey's face, already flushed with wine, turned a deeper crimson: plainly he hadn't expected his father to take this high moral tone. I could see that he was rattled; nonetheless he made a bold attempt to brazen it out.

"I consider they've no legal claim on me," he blustered. "They send in their bill, I pay it, and that's the end of it, so far as I'm concerned."

Mr. Greene's eyes were still fixed upon his plate, which contained a fragment of plum-pudding and a dab of brandy-butter.

"They may have no legal claim," he grunted, in a tone of distaste, "though it's a doubtful point. But I should certainly consider that they had a moral one."

Geoffrey drank off the rest of his champagne, and banged down the glass so violently that I thought it would break. There was a curious look in his eye—a furtive, almost a frightened look, which both shocked and surprised me. Could it be that Geoffrey—the family favourite, who could do no wrong, the athlete, the war hero and successful businessman—was afraid of his own father?

Madge, meanwhile—a rather ineffective buffer between the two disputants—had so far remained silent, glancing nervously from one to another. One could guess that her natural parsimony would incline her to take Geoffrey's part; on the other hand, she too was frightened of her father-in-law, and probably, for that matter, thought his judgment morally justified. Suddenly, with a bright little laugh, she turned to Mr. Greene.

"Oh, but of course Geoff'll pay eventually," she said. "He only meant to let them wait a bit for their money. After all, it *was* rather disgraceful—I can't stand inefficiency myself."

I saw Geoffrey look quickly from his wife to Mr. Greene: for a moment he seemed undecided—torn, as it seemed, between fear of his father and a natural reluctance to surrender his point. Madge's interpolation had plainly annoyed him, and the glance which he shot at her was anything but pleasant; for a moment I thought he was going to lose his temper. Then, with a sudden and rather theatrical assumption of *bonhomie*, he burst out laughing.

"Oh Lord, no—there was never any question of not paying them, naturally. In any case, it's the only garage in the place, and I can't afford to quarrel with 'em. But surely you'll agree, sir, that there's no harm in letting 'em wait a bit."

Mr. Greene, however, was not so easily mollified.

"I should send them a cheque tomorrow, me boy, if I were you," he said.

It must have been during the following summer—having descended, finally and ignominiously from the University—that I was present, much against my will, at a tennis party at The Grange. I didn't play tennis, but I was invited with my brother and sister (who happened to be at home), and my father expressed a wish that I should go.

The Grange, on a burning day in July, contrived to look hardly less depressing than in mid-winter. In the garden, the beds and borders were ablaze with ostentatious—and doubtless very expensive—flowers; the lawns, beautifully mown and liberally watered, rivalled those of Oxford itself; yet the hideous house and the gloomy conifers and monkey-puzzles which surrounded it cast a blight upon the sunlit scene. Making our way down to the tennis courts, we were received by Geoffrey, very much master of the occasion. My brother and sister were dressed for tennis, I was not; Geoffrey raised his eyebrows at my grey flannel suit, and I had to explain that I didn't play.

"What, not play tennis—a strapping young chap like you?" he exclaimed. Plainly he thought me extremely decadent, and only the fact that I was his guest prevented him from saying so.

I sat for the next hour watching the tennis: Geoffrey, as even I could see, was a first-rate player, Madge only so-so, and Nigel downright hopeless. After the first set or two, Nigel escaped from the court, and came and sat by my side.

"Oh God, isn't this *ghastly*," he exclaimed. "I do think families are hell, don't you?"

I agreed that, generally speaking, they were.

"I hear you've left Oxford," Nigel said. "Were you sent down?"

I admitted it, though the fact had so far been kept more or less a secret from our friends and relations.

"Geoff heard from some friend of his that you were going round with all the worst types of aesthete."

"Good heavens, who on earth told him that?"

"Oh, I don't remember his name—some rugger man he knows."

"I suppose Geoffrey imagines the worst," I said.

"I should think so—he usually does." Nigel glared at me resentfully. "Honestly, I've never known anybody so—so bloody censorious. Nothing's ever right that *I* do, I know that: he's always suspecting my motives, though I happen to know he's not so bloody virtuous himself. Thank God he's married, anyway—I couldn't have stood this house much longer with him in it. *Christ, how I loathe him!*"

Nigel hissed out this malediction so dramatically that it made me jump. I had known for a long time that he didn't hit it off with his brother, who obviously despised him and lost no chance of showing it; yet I was unprepared for such a vindictive outburst as this. Once started, Nigel continued for several minutes to pour out his woes: Geoffrey was a bully, a cad, a hopeless Philistine, he had always had the upper hand and he (Nigel) had never been given a chance.

Geoffrey, with Madge as partner, was at present playing an extremely fast and energetic game. At intervals there was a polite burst of applause from the spectators, which Geoffrey quite evidently enjoyed; he was rather vain of his appearance, and in his white flannels and open shirt did in fact look remarkably handsome. The curious thing was that Nigel, despite his violently expressed loathing for his brother, never for an instant took his eyes off him: he watched him, indeed, with a concentrated, feverish attention which, if he had not, but a moment since, assured me forcibly to the contrary, might have suggested that his feeling for Geoffrey was one of fanatical hero-worship, if not of passionate love.

That autumn I obtained a job of sorts with a large firm of wholesale booksellers. The chairman was a cousin of my father's, and it was thought that the work might suit my literary tastes, though in fact my job mainly consisted of lugging enormous piles of books up from the basement to the trade-counter. For these services to literature I was paid an "honorarium" of a pound a week.

During this period I was extremely lonely; I had lost touch with my Oxford friends, and knew few people of my own age in London. It was for this reason, I suppose, that almost by accident I slipped into a casual, half-reluctant friendship with Nigel Tufnell-Greene. I discovered that he caught the same train as myself in the morning, and we would travel up together. Soon we took to meeting for lunch, eating our frugal meal of baked beans or sausages at some Lyons' tea-shop or A.B.C. Sometimes, after work, we would meet in the station bar at Cannon Street, and drink a pint or two of beer. Nigel was still with his insurance firm, though threatening, as always, to walk out of it, and run away to sea. In fact, I think he regarded his work—as indeed I did mine—merely as an effective if tedious means of placating his parents, and I doubt if he ever seriously contemplated putting his threats into execution.

To tell the truth, I found Nigel a bore, yet in my loneliness I responded gladly enough to his friendly overtures, and even managed to persuade myself, in my more uncritical moments, that he really was the brilliant (though ill-starred) genius of his own imagination. I had a great capacity for romanticizing my friends, and I was willing enough, at the moment, to take Nigel at his own valuation; he might be bogus, but was I, after all, any less bogus myself? I liked to think of myself as a writer, but I knew, in my heart of hearts, that what I had so far written was poor stuff: facile pastiches of Aldous Huxley for the most part, without the least particle of originality.

I strongly suspected that Nigel was in much the same sort of position; nonetheless, he did at least provide me with someone to talk to. Bogus he might be, but at any rate he had—or pretended to have—a profound respect for Art, which was more than could be said for the people I knew at Blackheath or for my fellow-employees; and to me, at that age, anybody who even paid lip-service to art seemed preferable to someone who didn't. Nigel, moreover, really did want to paint or to compose music (he still seemed in some doubt as to the form in which his genius was ultimately to express itself); and who was I to say that his efforts—if only he could be freed from parental tyranny—would not one day be crowned with success?

In the train, at lunch or in the station bar, during that bleak and gloomy winter, we held endless and no doubt very enjoyable conversations about books, painting and music; though "conversation" is perhaps hardly the word to describe them, for they consisted, in actual fact, of a series of alternating monologues, having remarkably little connection one with another. Nigel would lecture me interminably about the "bah-lay", and I in my turn would hold forth about Proust, Cocteau or Gide. Our talk, however, was by no means confined to the subject of Art, for Nigel found a perennial satisfaction in discussing, in great detail and with malicious gusto, his home-life at The Grange. As I got to know him better, I found this disloyalty to his family less distasteful; I myself was passing through a phase of adolescent revolt, and frankly enjoyed Nigel's diatribes against parental authority and all the manifold horrors of "living at home". The Tufnell-Greenes, seen through the distorting lens of Nigel's imagination, seemed a monstrous caricature of my own family, a kind of multiple Aunt Sally upon whom I could work off, vicariously and without any sense of guilt, my own feelings of filial disaffection. In reality, our respective home-lives had little enough in common, for the Greenes, besides being immeasurably richer than my parents, were also far more autocratic, more snobbish and more rigidly conventional; nonetheless, I wholly sympathized with Nigel's attitude, and, like him, longed to be leading a free, Bohemian life in London—or, better still, in Paris.

On one or two occasions, at about this time, we spent an evening together in London. Nigel, despite his parents' wealth, was kept very short of money, though not so short as myself; neither of us could afford many gaieties, but by pooling our resources, we contrived to have a cheap dinner in Soho followed by a visit to a music-hall. Alcohol, I noticed, tended to make Nigel more gloomy and more acutely conscious of his own misfortunes than usual; on me it had the opposite effect, I became gay and sanguine, and I found Nigel, on the first of these occasions, rather poor company. By the end of the evening, however, he became more talkative, and our conversation took on a new intimacy. Not surprisingly, in the circumstances, we talked about Sex: I say "not surprisingly", for in those days, for young men like ourselves brought up in the middle-class, puritan tradition, the subject had an endless and obsessive fascination. The ice once broken, we continued to talk about it—with an enthusiasm in no way tempered by our extreme ignorance—whenever we met.

We tended, at first, to discuss the matter rather warily, and with a certain detachment; but it was not long before these discussions took on a more personal tone. Nigel, it seemed, after a night-out with one of his office acquaintances, had had what he referred to, portentously, as an Experience. I was duly impressed by this, and rather chagrined, for my own "experiences" had up till now been so partial and abortive as to be scarcely worth mentioning. Looking back, I suspect that Nigel's amorous activities were really quite as restricted as my own; he seemed, moreover (unlike myself), oddly undecided as to what, precisely, it was that he wanted. Nigel, I think, more than anything else, was obsessed by the *idea* of sex: a cloudy, ill-defined concept which seemed to be closely associated, in his mind, with the idea of being a genius.

Sometimes we would play the ribald game of picturing certain people—strangers, for the most part, seen in trains or in the street—engaged in the sexual act.

"Look at *him*" (or her, as the case might be), Nigel would suddenly hiss at me, pointing out somebody on the station platform at Blackheath. "Can you imagine *him* doing it?"

The game was often extended to include public characters or historical personages, and we agreed that it was very, very difficult to imagine the Victorians doing it at all.

"It must have been absolutely *ghastly*," Nigel would exclaim, with a horrified air. "Tumbling about in those great stuffy beds, in thick calico nightshirts—pitch dark, of course, and all over in no time: just hitching up their shirts and shoving it in."

I couldn't help feeling that this picture of Victorian domestic life might be slightly lacking in verisimilitude, and suggested as much.

"Can you imagine Queen Victoria *naked*?" Nigel would retort.

On occasion our licentious speculations would be brought to bear upon persons nearer home.

"Just think of Geoff and Madge," said Nigel. "The mind boggles."

I had to agree that it did. I could just manage to picture Geoffrey in the act, though it was not easy to visualize him in a position so lacking in dignity; but Madge defeated me entirely.

"I can imagine Geoff with *other* women," Nigel went on reflectively. "He's had mistresses, you know."

"Has he really?" I said, with a naïve surprise.

"Well, there were two or three girls he used to go around with; they weren't the sort he could marry, so it's pretty obvious he went to bed with them."

I found this, for some reason, difficult to believe: Geoffrey's air of conscious rectitude, his obsession with physical fitness, made such episodes seem incongruous and out of character; and for that matter, it was no uncommon thing, at that period—strange as it may seem today—for men like Geoffrey to remain virgin until their wedding-night. Nigel, however, was insistent upon the point.

"I'll bet you anything I'm right," he persisted. "In fact I know I am: I was in his bedroom, once, and I was fiddling about with his wallet, and there was a French letter in it."

"Before he was married?"

"Oh yes, long before."

Once, in an alcoholic moment, Nigel confessed to me that he cherished a passion for one of the choirboys at All Saints's Church, Blackheath. It was all very platonic, so Nigel assured me: a kind of hangover from a similar episode at school. I seized the opportunity to ask about his expulsion from Uppingham, but this, it appeared, had had nothing to do with choirboys; Nigel had, in effect, been superannuated, owing to his chronic inability to pass any sort of exam.

One Sunday morning I agreed to go to All Saints' with Nigel to view the object of his platonic passion (my parents were much surprised—as well they might be—by this sudden show of piety). Nigel had lately been afflicted by a mild attack of Anglo-Catholicism, from which, however (so he assured me), he had now quite recovered. All Saints' was extremely High, and was not patronized by the Tufnell-Greene family apart from Nigel (old Mr. Greene was a churchwarden at St. Michael's, which was Low; Molly preferred St. Margaret's, which might have been described as lower-middle-Broad). I could not, alas, muster much enthusiasm for Nigel's choirboy, a snotty child with ash-blond hair and prominent teeth, rather like a white mouse. I was more entertained by Nigel's behaviour in church: from habit, I suppose, he bobbed and bowed at every available opportunity, and seemed quite genuinely to enjoy the exercise.

Always with a slight feeling of reluctance, I found myself, during that winter and spring, slipping into a yet closer relationship with Nigel. We were never really intimate, our friendship remained a matter of habit and propinquity, but I came to accept him, at last, as part of my existence. I was still very lonely, and even a friend such as Nigel was better, I thought, than having no friend at all.

I even became, in due course, a fairly regular visitor at The Grange. Nigel, in the first instance, invited me rather apologetically.

"We needn't see much of the family, except at tea. I've got a room of my own, you know, upstairs.

Nigel's room proved to be a small, bleak attic at the top of the house. Theoretically, The Grange was centrally heated, but in practice the hot-water system didn't extend beyond the first and second floors, and Nigel's attic was always bitterly cold. Perhaps his father had exiled him to this comfortless abode in order to discourage his artistic ambitions; or perhaps Nigel himself had a romantic predilection for austerity—I could easily believe that he enjoyed thinking of himself as a penurious artist, pigging it in a garret.

Here, at any rate, Nigel was accustomed to immure himself, with his paints, his piano and his portable gramophone. Apart from these properties, the room was virtually unfurnished: there were two chairs, a ricketty table, no curtains and no carpet. Unframed canvases were stacked higgledy-piggledy against the walls; a pile of music lay untidily on top of the upright piano. The room could seldom have been dusted, and exhaled an atmosphere of staleness and accumulated dirt. From the small window, one looked out upon a prospect of funereal conifers, with a row of grim, cement-fronted houses beyond. Even in the summer, it must have been a cheerless enough place; now, in mid-winter, it was scarcely bearable. There was no fireplace, and it didn't seem to occur to Nigel to install an electric heater or even an oil-stove. Nigel might enjoy the austerity, but after my first visit I firmly refused to take off my overcoat.

Often, on a Saturday or Sunday, I would trudge over to The Grange and spend the afternoon in this gloomy *tour d'ivoire*; I must indeed, at that time, have been hard up for company, to endure such acute and such unnecessary discomfort. At half-past four we would descend to the luxurious, overheated drawing-room, and consume an enormous tea; I myself was disposed to linger over it, if only for the sake of being warm, but Nigel would hurry me upstairs again at the first opportunity.

"I'm sorry, but I just couldn't stand it a minute longer," he said, on one occasion when Geoffrey and Madge were up from Wrotham for the week-end. There had been several discreet references to Madge's "condition", for she was now pregnant.

"Can you *believe* it?" Nigel remarked bitterly, and proceeded to speculate once again, with a gratuitous obscenity, about his brother's sexual life. "I should think he does it with his eyes tight shut, and imagines she's Clara Bow," he finished.

I was getting bored, by now, with Nigel's sexual obsession; it was becoming increasingly difficult to discuss any other subject, and he was apt to revert, with a tedious insistence, to the married life of Geoffrey and Madge. He had developed a pathological loathing for his sister-in-law, with which I found it hard to sympathize; I didn't much like Madge myself, but she really wasn't such a harpy as it pleased Nigel to suppose. Listening to his ravings, one might have imagined him to be some disappointed spinster whom Geoffrey had jilted; there was in fact, I decided, something oddly spinster-like about Nigel's character—a harsh, resentful quality, at once prim and licentious, combined with a marked tendency to hysteria.

Meanwhile, since I had begun to frequent The Grange, I had at last been initiated into the mysteries of Nigel's creative activity. At my first visit he showed me a series of his pictures, exhibiting them with an air of detachment which too obviously masked a tremulous shyness. But if Nigel was embarrassed, so too—and perhaps even more painfully—was I; for the pictures were incredibly, pathetically bad. I was no expert, but even I could see that these dreary canvases possessed no merit whatsoever; to begin with, Nigel couldn't draw—his subjects, whether living or inanimate, were depicted with a childish crudeness, but without a child's spontaneity. There was no question of *fauviste* distortion, for most of the pictures were obviously meant to be representational; he just hadn't acquired the basic faculty for reproducing a given object in two-dimensional form. As for his colour, it was at once garish and curiously muddy: slapped on haphazard, often with a palette-knife, in an attempt, no doubt, to give an effect of dashing modernity. His subjects were mainly groups of figures, congregated in pubs or in the street; many of the pictures represented scenes of violence—soldiers fighting, children being run over, and so on. It was an unfortunate choice of genre, emphasizing as it did his ineptitude as a draughtsman; a few attempts at still-life, though technically no better than the rest, were at least less obtrusive in their badness, for apples and wine-bottles are, after all, somewhat easier to draw than the human body in violent motion.

As one inept canvas after another was propped up before me, I searched my mind wildly for something to say. I lacked the courage to tell Nigel that his pictures were downright bad; on the other hand, a certain native honesty inhibited the use of those facile compliments which would have been the easy way out.

Tossing the last picture into a corner, he turned to me and said abruptly:

"Tell me honestly, do you really think they're any good?"

I mumbled something to the effect that they showed great vitality and enthusiasm—which, in a sense, was true, for obviously Nigel had painted them *con amore*, and they were vital in the sense that the scenes which they portrayed were lively enough (or would have been, if he had been able to convey their liveliness).

Nigel, however, seemed anxious for a more positive judgment.

"Yes, but do you think they're really any *good*—d'you think I ought to go on painting?"

I hesitated, seeking desperately for some reply which should be at once inoffensive and relatively honest.

"I think," I said at last, "that you certainly ought to go to an art school."

Nigel's taut, anxious expression suddenly relaxed.

"I'm awfully glad you think there's something *in* them," he said.

I was silent, unwilling to point out that this was not, in fact, quite what I had said. I did indeed think that he ought to go to an art school, for if he insisted upon being a painter he might just as well try to acquire the elements of drawing and the manipulation of paint; that he had chosen to interpret my double-edged remark in a more flattering sense was, after all, no business of mine.

On a later occasion I asked Nigel to play me some of his musical compositions. I had little hope that they would be any better than his paintings, but it seemed unkind not to give him this much encouragement. As it happened, he proved more coy about his music than he had been about his pictures, and it was some time before I could persuade him to sit down at the piano.

"You've studied music since you left school, haven't you?" I asked, for I remembered Molly telling me once, when Nigel was out, that he had gone to the Blackheath Conservatoire.

Nigel looked at me blankly.

"Oh no, I've had no *training*," he confessed, with a little smirk which, I felt, implied a boundless contempt for all schools and academies; Nigel, evidently, was a firm believer in native wood-notes and the free airs of inspiration.

"I thought your mother said you were going to the Conservatoire," I said.

"I only go there to concerts, occasionally."

"I suppose you learnt music at school?"

"No, not really—I did start, when I was about fourteen, but the music-master was such an ass I gave it up. He made me play nothing but scales and five-finger exercises."

I was genuinely curious as to the results of this instinctive and quasi-Lawrentian approach to the thorny problems of harmony and counterpoint. But Nigel's wood-notes, when he was at last persuaded to warble them, were even more pathetic than I had expected.

His compositions were all written in the key of E flat major—though "written" is hardly the *mot juste*, for none of them had been committed to paper, and I doubt, in any case, whether Nigel was competent for such a task. He had taught himself, by ear, to thump out the stock jazz rhythm, and had picked up a few modern harmonies—presumably also by ear—from Stravinsky and Debussy. The result was a monotonous, syncopated banging, interspersed with slower passages, consisting mainly of chords of the whole-tone scale, though varied by occasional clumps of notes unrelated by any known rules of harmony. All his pieces—to which he had given such pretentious titles as "Symphonic Blues", "Harlem Nocturne", etc.—had, quite apart from their shared monotony of rhythm, this point in common: they all ended with a terrific cacophonous outburst, a chaos of chords and ill-executed arpeggios in which Nigel fairly let himself go.

Turning from the piano, after the last of these rhapsodic finales, he stared at me from his pale, myopic eyes with a pitiful mixture of pride and embarrassment.

"Very nice," I said feebly.

"Of course," he said, with a self-important air, "I write mainly in the jazz idiom, you know."

I said yes, I had gathered that he did, adding hastily that I really knew very little about music.

"Tell me honestly," he said, after a pause, "d'you think I ought to take up music seriously, or stick to painting?"

"I think if I were you," I said cautiously, "I should stick to painting."

Nigel looked gratified.

"As a matter of fact *I* think I've got rather more talent for it," he said.

He played a few irresolute chords, then banged down the lid of the piano.

"It's a funny thing," he said, "but when I play my own pieces, I always get a cock-stand."

This interesting confession led to a far-ranging discussion on the connection between sex and genius, two concepts which, for Nigel, seemed indissolubly associated. I soon became bored, but I was thankful enough to be spared further examples of Nigel's experiments in the "jazz idiom".

Poor Nigel, I thought, as I walked home across the Heath: he really was quite irreclaimably bogus. His "art", as I could now clearly perceive, was a mere neurotic compensation for his sense of inferiority. It was a common enough symptom of adolescence, yet with most people this compensatory striving after "self-expression" did at least spring from some basic grain of talent, whereas in Nigel's case it was, so to speak, *sui generis*: his art consisted entirely in the striving, without the least trace of innate ability. The sadistic paintings, the "rhapsodies" with their violent and discordant finales were for Nigel, as I could guess, so many symbols of revolt against the domination of his family, and more particularly of Geoffrey; the adult equivalents, in fact, of those hysterical tantrums to which he had been subject in his childhood.

As I got to know him better, I began to realize that Nigel, despite his rebellious attitude towards his family and all that they stood for, was in fact, when it came to the point, extremely conventional. In reality, he accepted and approved the traditional prejudices and standards of behaviour instilled into him by his parents, though it might amuse him to flout them; at heart he was a pure-bred Greene, whatever he might pretend to the contrary.

Physically, he had the same coarse-grained quality, the lack of any innate bodily refinement which characterized the males—and the females too, for that matter—of the Greene clan. At this time, too, his clothes were entirely conformist, copied more or less from those of Geoffrey: decent if somewhat loudly-patterned tweeds or, when in London, dark suits, black shoes and unobtrusive shirts and ties. His only noticeable concession to Bohemianism was his hair, which always looked as though it needed cutting, though what, in fact, it really required was not so much the barber's scissors as what my old nurse would have called "a good brush and comb". Mousily blond, it was always in a tangle, and looked rather greasy, as though he had brilliantined it but forgotten to brush it. His complexion, too, had a slightly greasy quality, as if he had just got out of bed and omitted to wash his face; he was afflicted, moreover, by blackheads and recurrent eruptions of acne.

His basic conventionality betrayed itself in a number of minor ways: he invariably, for example, wore a hat, and was perturbed because I sometimes didn't (hatlessness, at that date, had not yet become common among middle-class young men, except at the universities). In the summer, I would sometimes walk across Blackheath without a tie, and this also evoked his strong disapproval. And on one occasion, having cleared my throat of phlegm, I spat it out; we were quite alone in the middle of the Heath, but Nigel was inexpressibly shocked.

"No gentleman spits in public," he informed me in outraged accents.

"Perhaps I'm not a gentleman," I said.

"Don't be ridiculous, of course you are."

"I'm not so sure of that," I said teasingly. "My father's in trade, you know"—at which Nigel actually blushed, for all the world as though he were some prim spinster to whom I had announced that my father was in the lavatory.

On another occasion, we had strolled down through Greenwich Park to explore the Naval College and the riverside. On the way back, we passed a stall selling winkles, and without consulting Nigel I bought a bagful. Not only did I buy these plebeian delicacies but, with the pin provided, proceeded to eat them.

"But you *can't* do that," Nigel protested, in horror.

"What can't I do?"

"Why, eat those things—in the street—*with a pin*."

"You can't eat them *without* a pin," I pointed out.

We had started to walk up Croom's Hill, but Nigel now stopped in his tracks, too outraged, it seemed, to be seen in my company.

"You know perfectly well what I mean," he snapped. "It's bad enough eating winkles at all, but *in the street*!"

"I thought you were meant to be so unconventional," I jeered at him.

Nigel turned upon me furiously.

"So I may be, but damn it all, there are *limits*." He paused, at a loss for words; then, launching what he doubtless felt to be the heaviest bolt in his armoury, he added: "I should just like to hear what Geoff would say, if he could see you now."

I retorted, rudely, that I didn't care two hoots what Geoffrey would say, and walked on up the hill; Nigel, however, firmly refused to condone my ill-breeding, and trailed along, with an air of impassible dignity, at a distance of some twenty yards behind me.

It must have been at about this time that I first became friendly with Frankie Cartwright; I had met her, I suppose, in one of the Charlotte Street pubs, which I frequented occasionally when I could afford it. She was one of the few women I knew whom I could talk to as though she were a man, and a fairly sophisticated man at that; nor did I ever feel that she expected me to make love to her. She must, I suppose, have been about twenty-five or six, though to me, at twenty-one, she seemed older. A plumpish, placid and quite attractive girl, she was a Bohemian by temperament, though preserving, for the most part, a certain middle-class decorum in public; she drank a great deal, but could hold her liquor (as she was fond of saying) like a gentleman, and always looked clean and well turned-out. By profession she was a painter, trained at the

Slade, and exhibited occasionally with the London Group or elsewhere; she didn't, however, take herself very seriously as an artist, and supplemented her small private income by writing ephemeral but extremely efficient articles for the women's magazines. These activities were carried on—except in the summer, when she usually went abroad—in a pleasant early-Victorian house in Acacia Road, St. John's Wood.

At present Frankie was unmarried, having divorced or otherwise dispossessed herself of three somewhat difficult husbands. The first of these had been homosexual, the second an alcoholic and the third a heroin addict who had recently and rather conveniently died. These three marriages had really resulted from Frankie's social conscience, rather than from any erotic or romantic motive; her personal inclinations tended to involve her in a series of passionate affairs with members of her own sex, but where men were concerned, she was an inveterate do-gooder, with an incurable propensity for rescuing people from their Lower Selves. Fortunately, she had never shown any active signs of wanting to rescue me—perhaps she thought me beyond help—and we remained on the best of terms. I sometimes went to her parties in St. John's Wood, which had an agreeable way of going on all night; more than once, at daybreak, I had woken up to find myself sharing a camp-bed or divan with some young poet or painter whom Frankie had temporarily befriended. Her studio, which was large, contained a number of such useful articles of furniture, and these were usually found to be occupied, of a morning, by an assortment of similar couples, of varied and variable sex. I enjoyed these parties very much, though they usually resulted in a terrible hangover, due to the cheap Spanish wine with which Frankie commonly regaled her guests. One would wake in the morning to the dispiriting sight of rows and rows of empty bottles on the mantelpiece, but at half-past seven or so Frankie, with unobtrusive tact, would appear with an enormous tray of black coffee and prairie oysters, having consumed which her various *protégés* would be dispatched to their homes in a state of relative sobriety and euphoria.

*

One Saturday I had arranged to go to a film, in the evening, with Nigel, but that morning I was rung up by Frankie and invited to a party. I explained, rather dejectedly, that I had promised to go out with a friend.

"Why not bring him along too?" Frankie suggested. "The more the merrier."

Unwilling to forgo the party, I rather dubiously agreed to bring Nigel along. The party began late, and we had had several drinks before we arrived; after half an hour or so I observed that Nigel was rapidly getting drunk. He seemed, however, to be enjoying himself; a young ballet-dancer, called Billy Mavor, had turned up, and I could hear Nigel lecturing him, in his plummy voice and with a great air of authority, on the choreography of the *Firebird*—a subject upon which, I thought, the young man must surely be far more knowledgeable than Nigel.

Frankie, at this period, though vaguely left-wing, was not yet the ardent fellow-traveller she was later to become. Auden and Spender had scarcely begun to sound their rallying-calls, and Frankie, if she voted Labour (which I suspect was mainly a gesture of revolt against her parents), was in other respects uncommitted, and conversation at her parties was more likely to be concerned with the latest Virginia Woolf than with labour conditions in Jarrow or Ebbw Vale. With her more left-wing friends, Frankie would profess great pride in her plebeian origins: "Thank God I'm a proletarian," she would exclaim, with an air of rather smug satisfaction, though in fact she was nothing of the sort, for one of her maternal uncles was a lord, and her mother had married, for love, a poor barrister who, however, had afterwards become extremely successful. It was true that Frankie's paternal grandfather had been a provincial draper who had skimped himself to send his son to Oxford; but this, one felt, hardly justified Frankie's complacent claim to be proletarian by birth rather than by adoption.

"I think your friend's rather sweet, in a way," she remarked, encountering me momentarily in the crowd. "I suppose he's queer, isn't he?"

"I don't honestly know," I said. "In fact, I doubt if he knows himself."

"If you ask me, he likes people to think he is," Frankie said, "but *I* should say it's a case of every man his own wife—you know, a honeymoon in the hand's worth two in the bush."

Soon after this I happened to meet someone by whom I was attracted, and who—much to my surprise—reciprocated my feelings. We left the party together, though not before I had sought out Nigel, whom I found, by now, to be very drunk indeed.

Would he be able to get home all right, I asked, feeling a vague sense of responsibility, not so much on his account as on Frankie's.

"Christ, yes, I'm f-fine," he hiccuped. "It's a bloody good party. D'you know there's someone here who's actually danced in the *Firebird*?"

Saying good-bye to Frankie, I asked her whether she minded my leaving Nigel behind.

"Bless you, no," she assured me, "I'll put him to bed with a prairie oyster if he gets obstreperous." She eyed Nigel speculatively across the crowded room. "Poor lamb," she said, "he obviously hasn't learnt to hold his liquor. But don't worry. I'll deal with him."

Plainly, I thought, Frankie was looking forward to one of her rescue-operations.

I didn't, as it happened, see Nigel again for a week or two after this; apparently he had stayed the night in Frankie's house and returned home the next morning, much to the scandal of his family.

"I think Frankie's awfully nice," he said. "She wants to see some of my paintings."

In the spring of that year I was transferred to a bookshop (owned by the firm I worked for) in Old Broad Street. The shop was some little way from Nigel's office, and our meetings for lunch became less regular; nor did I see so much of him at Blackheath, for I had acquired—partly through Frankie—a number of friends in London, and was less dependent upon his company. We continued, however, to meet now and again; occasionally I would go to The Grange, where Nigel's attic was now, in the warmer weather, not quite so uncomfortable; or, less frequently, he would spend the afternoon with me in my own home. I gathered that he had become friendly with Frankie (with whom I myself had temporarily lost touch), and spent much of his time in St. John's Wood.

"I expect she's trying to rescue you," I said. "It's a way she has."

"I took some of my pictures to show her," Nigel said shyly.

"Oh, what did she think of them?" I asked, feeling a certain sympathy for poor Frankie, compelled to give a tactful verdict upon Nigel's pathetic canvases.

"She thinks", he said, "that I ought to go to an art school."

It was, I suppose, on one of his rare visits to my home that Nigel happened to notice, on the bookshelf in my bedroom, a copy of *The Well of Loneliness*. This book, during the previous year, had been vociferously attacked by James Douglas in the *Sunday Express*, and subsequently banned by the Home Secretary. Nigel immediately pounced upon it.

"Can I borrow this?" he asked.

"Yes, if you like," I said, "but you'll find it extremely dull."

I myself had scarcely been able to get through the book; Nigel, however, refused to be discouraged, and took it away with him.

On the following Saturday afternoon I received a visit from, of all people, Geoffrey. I was, as it happened, in bed with a slight chill, but Geoffrey, it seemed, wanted to see me urgently, and was shown up to my bedroom.

He bounced into the room and, without bothering to enquire after my health or even to pass the time of day, flung upon the bed my copy of *The Well of Loneliness*.

"I've brought back your book," he said tersely, and stood glowering down at me with an expression of outraged propriety, just as though I were an unmarried mother, and the book were my child of shame.

I thanked him nervously: he could hardly have come all the way across the Heath for the sole purpose of returning a book which I had lent his brother, and I wondered what was coming next.

After humming and ha-ing for a moment or two, he gave utterance to the following remarkable pronouncement:

"In future," he said, in a tone perfectly self-contained but obviously calculated to annihilate me, "in future I'd prefer that you didn't try and corrupt my brother with that sort of filth."

For a moment I stared at him, speechless with astonishment; then I burst out laughing.

Geoffrey frowned thunderously.

"I see nothing whatever to laugh at," he snapped.

"But it's perfectly ridiculous," I said, quite unable to keep a straight face. "Nigel asked if he could borrow the book, and I told him he could."

"I don't care whether he asked or not, it's a dirty book, and my father won't have it in the house, nor do I blame him." Geoffrey glared at me self-righteously. "I may say", he added, "that the pater's pretty sick about the whole business: if Nigel hadn't happened to say that the book belonged to you, he'd have flung it on the fire."

I looked at Geoffrey with mute incredulity: one had often heard of people performing this improbable action, but Miss Radclyffe Hall's novel was, after all, a notably bulky one, royal octavo, and running to some five hundred pages or more.

"But has he read it?" I ventured to enquire at last. "Have *you* read it, yourself?"

"Read it? Of course not. You don't think a decent man reads filth like that, do you?"

"But if you haven't read it, how do you know it's so filthy?"

"I read the papers, and that's quite enough for me."

"It happens to be an extremely dull and proper book," I said.

Geoffrey jerked his head impatiently.

"All I know is, it's about—er—unnatural vice, and if that's not filth, then I don't know what is." He gave me a withering stare. "As to what *you* choose to read, that's no business of mine; but I won't have dirty books like that left lying about at The Grange. Why, just suppose", he added, in horrified tones, "that my mother or Oonagh had happened to pick it up."

71

Suppressing a violent impulse to say that I would rather give Mrs. Greene or her daughter a copy of *The Well of Loneliness* than a bottle of prussic acid, I remained discreetly silent. I had expected that, after his brusque little homily, Geoffrey would depart; instead, he wandered across the room and stared out of the window.

"Nice little place you've got here," he said patronizingly. "Room for a tennis court, really—I wonder your pater doesn't lay one out. Look here," he turned upon me suddenly, "I wanted to ask you about Nigel."

"About Nigel?" I echoed vaguely.

"Well, you're by way of being a friend of his, and the fact is we're all a bit worried about him. It seems as if he can't settle down, somehow. This job of his, for instance: it's a good enough opening for a young chap, if only he'd pull his socks up and—and put some guts into it. The chairman's a friend of the pater's, you know, and he'd be quite prepared to look after Nigel, if only he'd show a bit of keenness. The trouble is, he won't: all he seems to think about is messing about with all this art stuff." Geoffrey paused, eyeing me questioningly. "D'you think, yourself, he's likely to do any good with it—painting, I mean?"

"I don't expect he'd ever make much money," I said, assuming that this aspect of the question was the one most likely to interest Geoffrey and his family.

"Oh, it's not so much a matter of money," said Geoffrey, rather to my surprise. "The question is, really, whether he's likely to be any *good*. You're an artistic sort of bloke yourself, you ought to know."

From an impulse of loyalty towards Nigel, I said that I thought he should be allowed to paint if he wanted to. Geoffrey didn't reply, but continued to stand at the window, twiddling the blind cord between his fingers. Something else, I guessed, was worrying him, besides Nigel's painting.

"The fact is," he went on, speaking almost as if to himself, "Nigel's a queer fish, and I can't make him out. He's not like an ordinary chap, doesn't play games, or do any of the usual things." Again Geoffrey paused, his eyes still fixed upon our lawn, as though measuring it up for a tennis court. "Has he got any girl-friends, that you know of?" he jerked out suddenly.

"He's quite friendly with a woman I know, Frankie Cartwright," I said. "She's a painter, too, and she thinks Nigel ought to go to an art school."

"Yes, I see," Geoffrey said, still with a preoccupied air, and eyeing me, I thought, with a vague distrust. He seemed on the point of saying something else; then, as though thinking better of it, he turned away towards the door. Pausing, with his hand on the knob, he barked at me, in orderly-room tones:

"Not a word of all this to Nigel, mind—it's just between you and me and the gatepost."

He gave me a brisk nod, and bounced out of the room.

After this, I prudently kept away from The Grange for some time, though—according to Nigel—the row over *The Well of Loneliness* had not, after all, been quite so dramatic as Geoffrey's account of it had led me to suppose. It had been Geoffrey himself who had discovered the book, and shown it to his father; Nigel had been summoned to the old man's study and given a mild scolding, but it was an exaggeration to say that Mr. Greene had threatened to hurl the offending volume into the flames. As it happened, I was glad enough to avoid The Grange, for I was becoming increasingly bored by Nigel, and dreaded having to make polite remarks about his pictures and his music.

One evening, about this time, I ran into Frankie in the Fitzroy.

"Oh, hullo, I've just been standing a drink to your boyfriend," she greeted me.

"Which one?"

"Why, you know—Nigel Greene. He was broke."

"That's nothing unusual."

"His parents have pots of money, he tells me. It does seem a shame he shouldn't be allowed to paint."

"Have you seen his pictures?"

"God, yes—they're ghastly: he's got about as much talent as

that pavement-artist in front of the National Gallery. Less, I should say."

"But he said you told him he ought to go to an art school."

"Well, so I did: it couldn't make him any worse, and it might make him a bit better. According to him, you seem to have given him the same advice, anyway."

"So I did—and for the same reason."

"After all, the poor lamb *wants* to paint, and it's a harmless enough occupation. And it would at least get him away from that frightful family of his. They sound the end."

"They are," I assured her, with feeling.

CHAPTER FOUR

Four Winds

In the year that followed I saw a good deal less of Nigel; not only had I other friends whose company I preferred, but I felt ill-at-ease at The Grange, which I avoided unless compelled to go there with my family. Nigel, moreover, gave up coming to our house; I imagine that he was hardly less nervous of my family than I was of his. My father, I knew, rather disliked him; he never said so, but in Nigel's presence he tended to assume a cold, withdrawn manner which, though not overtly offensive, was a sure sign of his disapproval.

My brother Cecil, who was in the family business at Folkestone, usually came up for week-ends, and on Sunday mornings, when my parents were at church (the Christian Science one, in Bennett Park), we would often have a pre-luncheon drink or two at a local pub called the Three Tuns. Nigel was also a fairly regular habitué, and it was upon this neutral territory that our meetings, nowadays, usually took place. The Three Tuns was much frequented by the local rugger fraternity, and sometimes, if he were at The Grange for the week-end, Geoffrey also would put in an appearance. He was not best pleased, as I could see, at encountering Nigel in these surroundings, and did his best to avoid his company; Nigel, however, refused to take the hint, and made a point of hob nobbing with the rugger crowd, among whom he would assume an unnaturally hearty air and drink a great deal of beer. My brother and I, sitting in a corner, derived much amusement from his antics; it was obvious that he wasn't really enjoying himself in the least, and I was prepared to bet that the chief purpose of this rather unconvincing display of *bonhomie* was to impress Geoffrey with his "normality" and his virile capacity for liquor.

More than ever, nowadays, he seemed to be gnawed by a perpetual resentment against his family and, it could be inferred, the world in general. The battle of the art school, I gathered, appeared to have reached almost complete deadlock; meanwhile, Nigel remained with his insurance firm, doing as little work as possible, and liable, as he seemed to think, to get the sack at any moment—a prospect which didn't perturb him in the least. I found his attitude of morose fatalism rather irritating, partly, perhaps, because I saw in it a reflection of my own ineffectual strivings to escape from a similar impasse.

"Why don't you cut loose and go right away somewhere?" I asked, adding—for I was going through a Rimbaud phase at this period—"Abyssinia, for instance?"

Nigel looked at me with a supercilious disdain, his pale, watery eyes glinting with malice.

"Why don't *you*?" he bleakly retorted.

The taunt was deserved: why, after all, didn't I? Partly, I suppose, because I was inclined to apathy, and liked my comforts; I was also, however, restrained by a genuine fondness for my parents, and an unwillingness to cause them distress. In Nigel's case, so far as one could judge, there was no such obstacle, and only, I felt, by some explosive and revolutionary gesture of this kind would he ever be able to free himself from the tyranny of his family. But Nigel, as I had often had occasion to observe, was at bottom thoroughly conventional, and in the long and inconclusive campaign against his parent's domination he was prepared to fight—as one might express it nowadays—only with conventional weapons.

It was, I think, in the early summer of the following year—1930— that I heard from my mother that Nigel was ill and had expressed a desire to see me. There was a curious air of mystery about this illness: it was not, for instance, given a name, and my family seemed slightly embarrassed when referring to it, as people are when cancer or T.B. is suspected. Was it very serious, I asked? No, it was nothing very bad, apparently: something, my mother thought, to do with the bladder.

With some reluctance and a mild curiosity I called, on the following Saturday, at The Grange, and was shown up to Nigel's room. When I entered it, the portable gramophone by his bedside was blaring out Milhaud's *Création du Monde*, so he could hardly, I inferred, be so ill as all that.

When he had stopped the gramophone, I asked him what was the matter.

"Oh, I've got a dose, that's all," he said, staring at me defiantly and with a trace of smugness, as though he were rather proud of his mishap.

"Good Lord, what *sort* of dose?" I exclaimed. "Not syphilis, I hope?"

"No, only clap, but it's quite unpleasant enough, I assure you."

"Do your people know?" I asked.

"Well, the doctor said he wouldn't tell them, but I expect they've guessed—at least, I should think the pater had. I told Geoff about it myself—he was as pleased as Punch."

"Why on earth should he be pleased?"

"Oh well, he thinks it's a proof that I'm normal, you see."

I had my doubts as to whether, medically speaking, this theory of Geoffrey's was a sound one, but said nothing. Nigel, I gathered, had had a particularly nasty time: instead of going to his family doctor, he had consulted a quack, with the result that he was now suffering from an inflamed testicle and an acute infection of the prostate (this, of course, was before the days of penicillin, or even of sulphonamides). Yet curiously enough he seemed to be, if not actually enjoying, at least deriving a certain gloomy satisfaction from his mishap. His illness, in fact—like his childish fits of temper or his adult aestheticism—seemed to represent yet another aspect of his perpetual yet ineffectual protest against his environment. The odd thought struck me that he had, perhaps, by some obscure self-destructive impulse, actually invited this latest misfortune.

I went to see him several times during his illness; on one of these visits, he greeted me with the news that he had been sacked from his job with the insurance company. The chairman of the firm had, it seemed, written a tactful letter to old Mr. Greene, pointing out that, since Nigel hardly appeared to have his heart in the work, he might be more usefully and profitably employed elsewhere.

"Fancy anybody putting their *heart* into insurance," Nigel exclaimed.

"What will you do now, do you think?" I asked.

"God knows—try and persuade the pater to send me to an art school, I suppose. Anyway, I won't have to go to that dreary office again, that's one blessing."

During Nigel's convalescence the battle of the art school was resumed, and finally, after a prolonged resistance—and much to everyone's surprise—Mr. Greene surrendered. Not, however, unconditionally: Nigel was to continue living at home, with an allowance of three pounds a week, and he was to attend the Goldsmith School of Art at New Cross, which had the advantage of being only two stations up the line.

After his enrolment at the school, some months elapsed before I saw him again; I was now working in a bookshop at Highgate, and had taken a bed-sitting-room in the King's Road, Chelsea. Then, one Sunday morning when I was spending the week-end at home, I encountered Nigel in the Three Tuns. Being now enfranchized, a full-blown art student at last, he wore corduroy trousers and a high-necked sweater, but in other respects seemed unchanged; Geoffrey was also present, and Nigel, as usual, was laying himself out to be hearty with the rugger crowd. When at last I managed to have a word with him, he explained that this was a sort of celebration: he had been forbidden alcohol for three months after his illness, and this sabbatical period had expired on the previous day. I asked him about the art school, but he replied rather vaguely, and seemed on the whole dissatisfied with the curriculum, which he found unenlightened and stuffy. I guessed that someone had been trying to teach Nigel a little about elementary drawing, and that he felt this to be *infra dig*. The teachers were one and all, according to him, "hopelessly academic".

"The other day, one of them was lecturing us about *Ingres*, of all dreary painters. Can you imagine anything more depressing?"

I pointed out that, though Ingres might be dreary, many people— including Mr. Clive Bell—thought him a pretty adequate draughtsman.

"Oh yes, from a purely *academic* point of view," said Nigel, who seemed to have got this word on the brain. "*Clive Bell*, indeed," he added, witheringly.

Nigel was by this time slightly drunk; it didn't take much to make him so, at the best of times, and he had, after all, been a total abstainer for several months.

"Tell you what," he said suddenly. "I promised I'd go down to Geoff's place next week-end. Why don't you come too?"

"Quite apart from anything else, I haven't been asked," I said.

"Oh, Madge'd love you to come. She's just joined this new thing called the Book Society, and she's gone terribly literary. The house is hell, you never get enough to eat or drink, but it's only for two nights, after all."

"What about Geoffrey?" I asked dubiously.

"Oh, I'll soon fix *him*," Nigel said, and thereupon led me up to the bar, where his brother was talking to a rugger man called Cridlan.

"Yes, rather, old boy," Geoffrey said, with beery *bonhomie*, when Nigel had made his suggestion. "Madge'll be frightfully bucked. You'll be able to talk to her about books and all that. I can buzz you both down on Saturday afternoon. I've just got a new bus, actually, rather a smart turn-out—I'm just running her in."

That week-end at Wrotham was to be the first of many such visits: a fact which, since I found the Greenes in general and Geoffrey in particular so antipathetic, may well seem surprising. The truth was that I was obsessed, at this time, by the idea of getting-into-touch-with-Reality; my Rimbaud phase was still in full swing, and Geoffrey, in so far as he was entirely extroverted, an athlete and a successful businessman, struck me as being more "real" (in the somewhat esoteric sense in which I was wont to employ the term) than most people I knew. All of which was doubtless very silly, though in those days, I suppose, among literary young men like myself—less tough and less illusion-proof than those of a later generation—such curious and unrewarding phantasies were of no uncommon occurrence. The prospect of spending a week-end with Geoffrey and Madge seemed to me scarcely less stimulating than taking a trip to Harrar or to the jungles of tropical America.

Geoffrey drove Nigel and me down to Wrotham on the Saturday afternoon, in his brand-new and very smart car. It was a windy, sunlit day in September, and after some weeks in London I found the drive through the suburbanized countryside agreeable enough. I had scarcely seen Geoffrey, apart from an occasional encounter in the Three Tuns, since the episode of *The Well of Loneliness*, and despite my new-born cult for him as a Man of Action, I felt decidedly nervous. He was, however, perfectly amiable, treating me with a man-to-man heartiness which, in a silly way, I found rather flattering. Perhaps, I thought, married life had mellowed him; or could it be, merely, that I myself had grown more tolerant?

The Greenes' house stood high on the chalk escarpment, backed by hanging beech woods, and facing south over the Weald. It was called Four Winds, and never was a house so appropriately named, for not only was its position extremely exposed, but—since Geoffrey had a passion for open windows—one lived in a perpetual draught. The house itself, I suppose, dated from about 1905: vaguely Tudor, and with mullions of that peculiar terracotta stone so typical of the period. One could imagine that it had been built by some enlightened Edwardian stockbroker, full of up-to-date ideas, who had read H. G. Wells and even, perhaps, knew the Garnetts over at Limpsfield. Its whole aspect seemed to proclaim, self-consciously, that it belonged to the twentieth century: a New Age of fresh air and bouncing optimism, of motor-cars and Bernard Shaw, Blériot and Votes for Women.

Madge received us with a great show of high spirits. She seemed, since her marriage, to have become excessively, almost unnaturally volatile: so much so that she found it difficult to remain motionless for a single instant. Tea was in process of being laid, when we arrived, by the parlourmaid, who seemed perfectly competent and well-drilled in her duties; yet Madge kept up an incessant and hypercritical commentary upon her every movement, and herself bustled quite unnecessarily about the table, shifting the teapot, rearranging the plates and so on. Madge, it seemed, rather resented the three or four servants which Geoffrey thought necessary for the running of the house, and would willingly, to save her husband's money, have dispensed with at least two of them and done the work herself. Since, however, the servants were there, she was determined to get her—or rather Geoffrey's—money's-worth, and spent much time in ensuring that the cook, housemaid and parlourmaid were never for a moment unoccupied.

Indoors, the house preserved the breezy, up-and-coming, early twentieth-century atmosphere suggested by its exterior. The mullioned windows had leaded panes, inset with little panels of stained glass: galleons in full sail, Tudor roses or *art nouveau* water-lilies. The green-tiled hearth was surmounted by a chimney-piece of unstained oak; of oak, too, were the doors and the panelling. The furniture itself had come, I should guess, from Heal's: Madge's taste was not very enterprising, but in its rather obvious, "Homes and Gardens" style, the room gave a pleasant enough if not a very restful impression.

Filled with a transient euphoria, induced by the drive, the prospect of tea and the prevailing atmosphere of rather shrill conviviality, I was prepared to be well-disposed towards everything and everybody, and complimented Madge, somewhat effusively, upon the house, the drawing-room and the view over the Weald.

"Yes, it really *is* rather jolly, isn't it?" Madge replied, with satisfaction.

A better word could hardly, I felt, have been chosen to describe Four Winds. Both in its furnishings and in the way of life prevailing among its inmates, jollity was the dominant note; the chintzes were jolly, so was the carpet, and Madge laughed and joked incessantly. There was, moreover, a certain quality of improvisation about the Greene *ménage* which increased this impression; despite the servants, the up-to-date comforts and the whole paraphernalia of a well-off middle-class household, life at Four Winds had the slapdash, come-as-you-please air of some prolonged and elaborate picnic. Every small mishap evoked shrieks of merriment, the ordinary domestic routine, one felt, was only maintained by an unceasing struggle (on Madge's part) against overwhelming odds.

Tea was rushed through at a great pace, for Geoffrey was in a hurry to get out of doors; meals at Four Winds were invariably hustled, perfunctory affairs, and usually for the same reason. Two dogs, a Sealyham and a bull-terrier, leapt and careered about the tea-table, alternately scolded and gushed over by Madge. Geoffrey, who seemed in a very good humour, related a number of sailing anecdotes—he now possessed a small boat of his own, which he kept in the harbour at Gillingham. It was not a reposeful meal. Geoffrey, having gulped his tea, rushed out into the garden: he had a job to do on the car, a gate needed repairing, he wanted to have a word with the gardener. It was time the roses were pruned, he added: perhaps we blokes might give him a hand in the morning? At this point, Madge's child, Tony, now about eighteen months old, was brought downstairs by his nanny for our inspection: he was a robust little boy, taking after Geoffrey, and supplying (I reflected) an incontrovertible proof that the marriage of Geoffrey and Madge had actually been consummated: a circumstance which Nigel and I, a few years ago, had professed to find altogether incredible.

Madge gushed over her offspring for just so long as, no doubt, she thought suitable; she was not really, I guessed, very fond of children, and probably preferred dogs. Nigel and I were invited, in our turn—by the nanny, rather than Madge—to gush, and after ten minutes or so the child was removed to the nursery. Madge, excusing herself, shortly followed them upstairs, and Nigel and I were left, for a few minutes, in peace.

But not, as it happened, for long: soon Geoffrey's voice was heard shouting for Nigel to come and help him jack up the car. Nigel trotted off obediently to the garage, and, left to myself, I took the opportunity to examine the room—which Geoffrey called the lounge—with a somewhat closer attention. The pictures, like the rest of the house, struck a prevailingly jolly note: there were a few hunting prints, some dogs by Cecil Aldin, and two screamingly funny drawings (also of canine subjects) by Alfred Leete. Less jolly, and perhaps representing Madge's more highbrow inclinations, were some tasteful sketches of wild geese flying over marshes; there were also some anonymous, rather auntish water-colours, and some mottoes in poker-work ("ghoulies and ghosties", and some lines by R.L.S.). Dispersed among these were one or two admirable Japanese prints, which had probably come from The Grange; and, tucked away in a corner, where it couldn't be seen, a small seascape by Boudin which, as I learnt subsequently, had been a wedding present from old Mr. Greene.

The bookshelves, too, were instructive: a few books on fishing and sailing represented Geoffrey's contribution to the family library; the rest were obviously Madge's. There were a few leather-bound Tennysons and Brownings, and *Poems of Today* (First Series); a row of novels, including *The Forsyte Saga, The Young Enchanted, Portrait in a Mirror* and E. M. Delafield's *Diary of a Provincial Lady* (a recent Book Society choice). A smaller shelf accommodated a collection of Nelson's "sevenpennies", relics no doubt of Madge's girlhood: Baroness von Hutten, C. N. and A. M. Williamson, Rita, etc., etc. There was also a nearly complete collection of the works of Gene Stratton Porter. Among more recent imports I noticed, to my surprise, a novel about public school life, *Tenants of the House*, by Denzil Pryce-Foulger, who happened to be an acquaintance of mine. This I found intriguing: it was not, I felt, quite up Madge's street, but still less could it be up Geoffrey's.

My researches were soon cut short by a summons from Geoffrey: my help was needed in the garage. For the next hour or so I was kept busy doing odd jobs and running errands for my host. In normal circumstances, I should have strongly resented his assumption of authority, and the menial tasks I was required to perform; but Geoffrey, almost overnight, had become a hero-figure, the incarnation of my cult for the strenuous life, and I positively enjoyed—in inverted commas, so to speak—being bullied and ordered about by this handsome and athletic extrovert.

At last, grubby and sweating, we returned to the house. Here we were greeted by Madge with a renewed outburst of jollity.

"I don't know how you boys feel about it," she exclaimed, clapping her hands together, and with a roguish gleam in her eye, "but *I* think it's time we all had a little drink."

We boys thought this a jolly good idea. How nice the Greenes were, and how wrong I had been, I thought—with the penitent ardour of a convert—to despise them. An afternoon of healthy exercise, followed by a jolly, convivial evening—what could be more delightful? The Greenes might not be very cultured but, I decided, they knew how to live.

Glasses were produced, and a decanter of sherry; Madge poured it out, still with an air of reckless conviviality, though I noticed that my glass, when she handed it to me, was only two-thirds full.

"Cheers!" said Madge, and "Mud in your eye!" said Geoffrey. I drank my sherry rather quickly, then waited, hopefully, for my glass to be refilled. Madge, however, sipped her drink very slowly indeed, and seemed determined to ignore my empty glass. Perhaps, I thought—after twenty minutes had passed—we were meant to help ourselves; nobody else, however, made a move to do so, and I felt nervous of taking the initiative. At last Madge finished her sherry, collected our glasses, and placed them on the tray with the decanter.

"Well, that *was* nice," she said gaily. "And now I simply *must* pop along to the kitchen and see that cook doesn't over-cook the cauliflower *au gratin*. She's really hopeless, one can't leave her to do a single thing."

Madge departed, carrying the tray with her. My hopes for a merry alcoholic evening were dashed; nor did they revive when we went in to dinner, for instead of the bottle of claret or burgundy—or even of champagne—which I had confidently expected, the only fluid which graced the table was a large and forbidding-looking jug of water. After the soup, Geoffrey did propose a bottle of beer, though Madge, I noticed, looked askance at the suggestion. The beer was produced at last—a pint of pale ale shared out between Geoffrey, Nigel and myself.

This stinginess—at least on Geoffrey's part—surprised me, for the Greenes, as a family, were far from abstemious, and Geoffrey, after all, was in the wine trade. I was disappointed, but, borne up by my enthusiasm for this hearty and extrovert *vita nuova*, managed to enjoy the evening well enough—or at least to persuade myself that I was doing so. The dinner itself was well-cooked, but there was not quite enough of it, and Madge was inclined to be forgetful about second helpings. Afterwards we sat in the drawing-room and listened to the wireless: Nigel particularly wanted to hear a Sibelius symphony which was being performed. When we had tuned into the concert, Madge assumed a rapt expression (though continuing to ply her knitting-needles); Geoffrey, however, far from looking rapt, gave a snort of contempt.

"What's that—the tune the old cow died of?" he loudly inquired. A minute or two later, after much noisy rustling of *The Times*, he sprang to his feet and, muttering something about "making sure that he had filled up with oil", escaped once more to the garage.

The symphony over, Madge and I embarked upon a literary conversation. Did I belong to the Book Society, she asked?

"I think they really choose awfully well," she said. "Of course, one doesn't want to be spoon-fed, I know, but after all there's always an alternative choice. Naturally, I belong to a library as well, though honestly there's so much to do, I don't seem to get much time for reading, nowadays."

Literature occupied us for half an hour or so, and before long it was bedtime. The Greenes retired sharp at half-past ten, and since there seemed no prospect of getting anything else to drink, I was glad enough to go myself. Geoffrey and Madge, I reflected— still with my convert's enthusiasm—were really very sensible to be so self-denying: drink was a great waste of money, and why give oneself a headache in the morning? Nonetheless I longed for a drink at this moment; nor was my craving diminished by the suspicion that Geoffrey—when he returned, ostensibly from the garage—had just been having one. I could have sworn that his eyes were brighter, his cheeks more glowing, than when he left the room; perhaps it was only the fresh air, but, as he passed my chair, I caught a whiff of something curiously like whisky.

Next morning all was bustle and confusion at Four Winds: one might have supposed that the entire household was to set forth, that very day, upon some bold and probably desperate enterprise. All that was, in actual fact, involved was that Madge had expressed a desire to go to church in the neighbouring village; but the plans and changes of plan, the suggestions and counter-suggestions consequent upon her inopportune announcement, kept everybody fully occupied for more than an hour after breakfast. It struck me as odd and out of character that these practical, efficient people, faced by a minor domestic problem, should make such a to-do; my own family would have settled the matter in no time, but for Geoffrey and Madge it seemed likely at any moment to blow up into a major emotional crisis; they could hardly, I thought, have made more fuss if they had been characters in some play by Tchekov.

Madge was not a very regular churchgoer, but liked to go on special occasions; today, as it happened, was the Harvest Thanksgiving, and she had more or less promised the rector that she would be there. Geoffrey, for his part, had planned a trip over to Gillingham to show Nigel and myself his new boat; but Madge could hardly be expected to walk to church, a distance of over two miles, though she could, she thought, almost certainly get a lift back. To take Madge to church would obviously wreck Geoffrey's day, and this he made perfectly clear; on the other hand, he would not hear of Madge omitting her devotions. For his part, as he confided to Nigel and me (Madge being momentarily out of earshot), he hadn't much use for "organized religion"; it was a good thing in its way, no doubt, but if a chap was made of the right stuff, and had been properly brought up, he ought to be able to keep straight without a lot of pious mumbo-jumbo. Besides, working in an office all the week, as he did, he needed fresh air at the week-end; and in any case, he didn't like the local padre, who was High.

Madge, as it happened, didn't like the padre much either, but one had, she said, certain obligations; on the other hand, she was perfectly willing to miss church if it was going to be a bother.

"Actually, I'd simply love to go over to Gillingham with you lads," she protested.

"No, no, my girl," retorted Geoffrey, with an air of chivalrous martyrdom, "if you want to go to church, I'll run you over, naturally."

"Oh but *honestly*, Geoff——"

"No, no—we'll drop you off at the church, and then I'll take these two lads for a spin. We might even have a noggin at the King's Arms before lunch—that is, if you're sure of getting a lift back."

Finally Madge surrendered, and Geoffrey was allowed to assume his martyr's crown. There followed a strenuous hour's work in the garden, pruning the rambler roses: a job which enabled Geoffrey, wearing leather gloves and armed with a pair of secateurs, to work off a good deal of his bad temper. When the time came to set forth, Nigel decided that he wouldn't come with us after all; he wasn't, he said, feeling very well.

Geoffrey and I, having dropped Madge at the church, drove leisurely along unfrequented roads, waiting for the pubs to open. It was another brilliant morning, the countryside was delightful, and I felt well-disposed towards everything and everybody—including Geoffrey's conversation. For a solid hour he discoursed to me upon sailing, fishing, his rugger team and the activities of the Territorial battalion to which he belonged (Geoffrey was a very keen Territorial—"we're bound to have another go at Jerry sooner or later"—and grumbled to me at great length because Nigel firmly refused to become one too). A few months ago I should have found such disquisitions merely exasperating; now, however, I lapped them up (though, to tell the truth, I had but the faintest idea what he was talking about) as the simple, unaffected utterances of a man of action.

The King's Arms, where we went for our "noggin", was a pub of a type which, common enough today, was at that period something of a novelty. It was kept by an ex-officer of the Flying Corps, who had tarted it up in the Waring and Gillow Olde Englishe style of 1925, with the avowed aim of attracting what he called "a better class of people", by which he meant the commuting City men and stockbrokers in the neighbourhood, as opposed to the local rustics who had previously frequented it, and who had now been driven elsewhere. There were a lot of fake-Tudor beams (though the original building was in fact early Victorian), horse-brasses and warming-pans; the Saloon Bar had been rechristened the Buttery, and was hung with tasteful prints of hop-pickers and oast-houses. The stockbrokers had duly fallen for these attractions, and the bar, as we entered it, was loud with their hearty haw-hawings and the competitive shrieking of their wives.

"Decent little place, this," said Geoffrey, when we had ordered our tankards of bitter and sat down, rather uncomfortably, at a small table in a corner. "I like the old-world atmosphere, myself—awfully jolly, really. Fellow who keeps it's a gent, too, it's the sort of place you can bring your wife. Madge and I quite often come."

I had a sneaking fondness for old-world atmospheres myself (though I was wont to pretend that I knew better), and in my present besotted state was quite prepared to agree that the King's Arms was very nice; I could even condone what might have seemed to me, in a more rational mood, Geoffrey's snobbish remark about the proprietor (whose gentility, for that matter, struck me as being open to question). Soon I went up to the bar to refill our tankards. Over our second pint, Geoffrey's manner became noticeably more relaxed; I had seldom if ever known him so genial. The crowd of "better class people" was becoming denser every moment; occasionally Geoffrey would greet one of them with an off-hand joviality—"Hullo, Charles, old boy—hullo, Everard"—though he didn't ask any of them to join us. After a few more jaunty observations about the King's Arms and its old-world charm, he leant confidentially across the table.

"Fact is," he said, "I'm rather glad to get you to yourself—I wanted to have a bit of a talk to you about Nigel."

"What about him?" I said cautiously.

Geoffrey paused for a moment before he replied.

"He seems to have picked up some pretty queer friends at that art school of his," he said at last.

Having met none of Nigel's fellow-students, I was unable either to confirm or deny this.

"Queer in what way?" I asked curiously.

"Oh, weedy-looking sort of blokes, with long hair. Look as if they could do with a bath, most of 'em. Of course, it's no business of mine—if the pater's prepared to give Nigel his head, I've no more to say." This, as I could guess, was a mere fashion of speaking; in reality, Geoffrey had a lot more to say, and now proceeded to say it. What Nigel really needed, he declared, was discipline: "A couple of years in the Army might have licked him into shape, but it's a bit late to start thinking of that." Failing the Army, he ought to have a regular job of some kind—"to keep him out of mischief".

I was tempted to remark that Nigel's insurance job had conspicuously failed in this object, but refrained.

Geoffrey cleared his throat nervously.

"You know, of course, that he—er—had a dose?"

I nodded.

"You don't know, I suppose, how he came to pick it up? I mean—er—what sort of person?"

I said, quite truthfully, that I didn't, for Nigel had been surprisingly reticent on this point.

"Well, all I can say is, I don't think much of the sort of crowd he goes around with. There was a chap he brought along to the Tuns one Sunday—greasy little tyke, like a wop, and I could swear he had powder on his face. To tell you the truth, I was just itching to kick the little swine up the arse."

Remembering the affair of *The Well of Loneliness*, I could guess where the conversation was leading: the cat, so to speak, was already half out of the bag, and I wondered how long it would be before Geoffrey finally brought himself to release it.

At that moment he interrupted himself to refill our tankards. I was rather surprised at the amount he was drinking, and wondered what Madge would have had to say on the subject.

"By the way," he announced, with apparent irrelevance, when he had returned to the table, "I was reading a book the other day."

This in itself was a surprising statement, for I had never before heard of Geoffrey doing any such thing.

He paused, then added:

"It was a book Nigel brought down, actually—all about life at a public school, by a fellow called Pryce-Foulger."

Rather unwisely, perhaps, I said that I had read the book, and that the author was an acquaintance of mine.

"What, you know the feller, do you?" Geoffrey eyed me with a mixture of disapproval and a slightly prurient curiosity. "I suppose he's one of these—er—nancy-boy types, eh?"

"I should hardly say so," I said.

"But good Lord, man, he makes it perfectly plain—I mean, damn it all, he actually mentions—" Geoffrey broke off, and swallowed a long draught of beer. Now that the cat was well and truly out of the bag, he looked suddenly embarrassed.

"All I can say is, it's the filthiest muck *I've* ever read," he went on. "The only reason I mentioned it was because—well, the fact is, I'm a bit worried about Nigel, and so is the pater. You don't think *he's*—er—one of those, do you?"

"Who, Nigel?"

"Yes, Nigel," Geoffrey snapped, rather irritably.

"He's never told *me* so," I said coolly.

"Yes, but what do you think yourself? Damn it all, you're a friend of his."

"I've not the least idea," I said.

"Well, all I can say is, if I thought a brother of mine was like that, I'd—I'd—" Once again Geoffrey broke off abruptly, banging his tankard down on the table; his face had gone scarlet, and I could see that his hands were trembling. "I just can't *stand* all that sort of thing," he went on at last. "Chaps like that ought to be strangled at birth . . . Mind you, I don't believe for a moment that Nigel's really that way, but if I thought that any of his friends—" Geoffrey gave me a rather nasty look, then hastily buried his nose in his tankard. "Come to that, strangling's too good for such swine:

if I had anything to do with the government of this country, I'd pass a law to have 'em all castrated. And what's more, by God, I'd be the first to offer my services."

Geoffrey took another drink, then said, in a more normal tone:

"Funny that bloke's name should be Pryce-Foulger. I suppose you don't know if he's any relation of the rugger man—the one who played for Oxford last season?"

I said that Denzil Pryce-Foulger had himself played rugger for Oxford.

Geoffrey looked so flabbergasted that I nearly burst out laughing.

"D'you mean to tell me that the fellow who wrote that book was the same Pryce-Foulger who scored those two tries against Cambridge in the Varsity match?" he barked at me incredulously.

I assured him that such was the fact.

"Well I'm damned, I just wouldn't have believed it."

I offered him another pint, and rather to my surprise he accepted it. The truth was, as I was beginning to realize, that Geoffrey's apparent abstemiousness was merely a concession to Madge, who, though she liked to, appear broadminded and even "unconventional" about alcohol, was in fact much too parsimonious to drink—or to tolerate other people drinking—much more than a single glass of sherry, beer or whisky at a time.

When I had bought the drinks, Geoffrey began to question me again about Denzil Pryce-Foulger. The fact that Denzil, a rugger blue, should have written a novel at all—let alone one which dealt with unnatural vice—had plainly upset all his preconceived ideas.

"But look here," he insisted, "is the fellow a bugger or is he not?"

I said that I really knew very little about Denzil's private life. Geoffrey, however, continued to glare at me with an expression of complete stupefaction, bewildered, perhaps, by the unfortunate verbal echo: to think that rugger should ever be associated, however remotely, with somebody who, to all intents and purposes, had proclaimed himself a bugger! Confronted by his wide-eyed *naïveté*, I found it more and more difficult to control my laughter; fortunately he soon changed the subject, via Pryce-Foulger, to the prospects of his own rugger club during the coming season. Shortly afterwards, happening to look at his watch, and finding it later than he had thought, he hurried me out of the pub.

"Mustn't be late for lunch," he said briskly.

As we climbed into the car, he gave me a sidelong, slightly furtive glance.

"I wouldn't say too much to Madge about—well, about the King's Arms," he muttered, shamefacedly. "That's to say, it's perfectly all *right*, of course, she goes there herself, but she doesn't hold with a lot of boozing, and—well, four pints might strike her as a bit excessive, d'you get me?"

The rest of that week-end passed, for me, in a daze of unaccustomed and mainly violent activity. In the afternoon, Geoffrey continued to prune the roses, assisted by myself and watched by Nigel, rather wanly, from a deckchair (poor Nigel had confessed to me, unhappily, after lunch, that he "thought he had had a relapse"). My job was to carry the prunings down to the bottom of the garden and burn them on the bonfire; Geoffrey, wearing only shorts and a singlet, worked like a demon—perhaps by way of counteracting the morning's indulgence. The afternoon was warm though with a pleasant tang of autumn; soon I was in a muck-sweat, and rather enjoying it. By tea-time I had attained a notable pitch of euphoria, and rather surprised Madge by my repeated assurances of how much I was enjoying the week-end. It was true enough, in a way; but I should have been hard put to it to explain, to Madge or Geoffrey, the precise nature of my enjoyment.

Geoffrey drove Nigel and myself up to London early the next morning.

"You simply *must* come again," said Madge gaily, from the doorstep, and I found myself promising to do so with an enthusiasm which, at that moment, seemed to me perfectly genuine.

Back in the King's Road, that evening, I continued to assure myself that I had greatly enjoyed the week-end; and on the following Saturday, at home at Blackheath, I confided as much to my parents, who looked surprised—as well they might—by this latest eccentricity of mine, though they seemed, on the whole, to approve of it. My brother, also home for the week-end, demanded to know every detail of what had occurred at Four Winds; he was extremely amused by my latest *culte*, and before long I was sharing his amusement. Seen from his detached and decidedly frivolous viewpoint, the Greene household had, as I was bound to admit, its comic side.

A fortnight later I spent another week-end at Four Winds, and thereafter, for the next six months or so, became a fairly frequent visitor. This was partly due to Nigel, who spent a good deal of his time there and—as I guessed—valued my services as a buffer. His own visits were prompted partly—as indeed were mine—by a desire to escape from his own home, partly by the fact that, being on the water-wagon, he felt Four Winds to be a refuge from temptation. For Nigel's fears had been confirmed: he had suffered a relapse, probably as a result of that premature celebration at the Three Tuns, and was now condemned to an indefinite period of abstinence, accompanied by bi-weekly prostatic massage. This frustrating and painful régime was to endure, with intermittent lapses, for the next five or six years; due to initial neglect, his infection had become chronic, and during the period which he passed at the Goldsmith School he was never really well. Whatever Geoffrey's feelings may have been in the matter, I think that Madge was genuinely sorry for him; certainly she asked him repeatedly to Four Winds, and he seemed glad enough—despite his dislike for her—to go. He had, I gathered, ceased to frequent St. John's Wood for the time being, doubtless finding the alcoholic atmosphere of Frankie's *ménage* too much of a strain upon his good resolutions.

When in my brother's company, I continued to regard these visits to Four Winds largely as a joke: I saw them, so to speak, as so many parentheses in my life, incongruous sorties into a phantasy-world which my brother and I referred to as "Greene-land". I would laugh at Geoffrey and Madge, and maliciously retail, for my brother's benefit, every detail of their utterances and their social behaviour; yet my romantic predilection for Four Winds and its inmates remained, for a matter of eighteen months or two years, a kind of private, inadmissible cult which, though at times I recognized its absurdity, I couldn't bring myself finally to abandon. As personalities in their own right, the Greenes failed to make any real impact upon me, for the very good reason that my conception of them was largely the product of my own imagination. I saw them, in fact, as potential characters in that vast Proustian novel which I hoped one day to write: puppets of my own creation to whom I attributed qualities which, in real life, the Greenes conspicuously lacked. As living people, they remained, so far as I was concerned, "flat" characters; and, as such, it was hardly surprising that, having ceased to play the romantic and almost wholly fictitious parts for which, as a novelist, I had cast them, they should soon be forgotten.

Partly, perhaps, as a result of my brother's teasing, partly as the consequence of a growing aptitude for destructive self-analysis, I began in time to realize that such phantasy-weaving was not only extremely silly but a great waste of time. Yet I continued to accept Madge's invitations, and if my hero-cult for Geoffrey had lost much of its original potency, I did retain a sort of affection, based upon habit and association, for the breezy and faintly Bedalian atmosphere of Four Winds. Like Helen Schegel in *Howards End*, I was more than half-aware of the "panic and emptiness" that lay behind the solid-seeming façade of good manners and conventional domesticity; yet I continued to relish, with a conscious perversity, the trappings of a way of life which, in saner moments, I both feared and despised.

The Greene façade, for that matter, was beginning at this period to show signs of cracking: relations between Geoffrey and Madge were becoming strained, and on more than one occasion Geoffrey had lost his temper with his wife in my presence. Nor was the situation much improved, apparently, by the birth of Madge's second child, a girl, which occurred at about this time. A growing atmosphere of tension pervaded the house, and I was more than once visited by vague premonitions of coming disaster.

It was at about this time that a small incident occurred which gave me a further and not very pleasant insight into the domestic life of The Grange. I had been dining in London with a friend, and had gone to a play; afterwards we went to the Criterion *brasserie* for a drink. For some reason we entered the building not by the back entrance (which led directly to the *brasserie*) but by the front one, so that we had to pass through the upstairs restaurant. As we mounted the steps, a couple emerged from the interior, through the revolving doors; standing aside to let them pass, I was vaguely aware of a rather vulgar-looking old gentleman accompanied by a young woman who, only too obviously, was no better than she should be. Another party followed upon their heels, delaying our own entrance, so that I found my glance returning to the old man and his companion, who were waiting on the bottom step while the commissionaire called a taxi. I had been struck by something vaguely familiar about that bald head and underhung jowl; a second glance told me that it was none other than old Mr. Herbert Greene.

Fortunately he hadn't seen me, and a moment later we passed through the door into the restaurant. I could hardly believe that the old gentleman I had seen was really Herbert Greene, owner of The Grange and churchwarden at St. Michael's; or, if he were, that his companion had actually belonged to the category in which, at first glance, I had immediately placed her. Yet I knew, beyond a doubt, that it had in fact been Mr. Greene, and I was equally certain that his lady friend was not—as I had tried vainly to persuade myself—some niece or cousin, a respectable member of the Greene clan, whom he happened to have been taking out to dinner.

I found the episode rather shocking. It wasn't so much that I specially disapproved of old Mr. Greene's conduct—which struck me, in any case, as being ludicrous rather than morally repellent—as that my preconceived ideas about the family had been suddenly upset. I knew the Greenes to be vulgar and aggressively Philistine, coarse-grained in temperament as they were in body; I knew, moreover, that the males of the clan were highly-sexed and more than normally philoprogenitive. Yet I had naïvely believed them to be, so far as their sexual habits were concerned, the soul of respectability. In youth, no doubt, they had sown a few wild oats, as Geoffrey (if Nigel were to be believed) had done before his marriage; once married, however, they became—or so I had been, up till now, convinced—*rangés*, fathers of families, and restrained by the sheer force of convention and family tradition from straying beyond the conjugal fold. That old Mr. Greene should be taking a tart home to bed with him would not, if I had been rather more sophisticated, have seemed very surprising; as it was, it shocked me as profoundly as though I had encountered my own father in a similar situation.

It must have been in the late autumn or early winter of 1932 that I spent what was to be the last of my many week-ends at Four Winds. There was no indication, at the time, that this visit (though it was to prove a disturbed and not very happy one), was in any way final; yet I did, I think, have a vague prescience that a phase of my life was coming to an end. Perhaps it was, merely, that my factitious and purely literary enthusiasm for "Greene-land" had run its course; certainly, of late, I had found myself markedly less susceptible to the charm of Four Winds, and increasingly aware of the emptiness which lay behind it. Madge had become more shrill and inclined to nag, her face wore a chronic expression of taut anxiety, as though she were perpetually steeling herself to expect the worst. Geoffrey had also undergone a change, and not for the better: he too seemed constantly on edge, and would flare up into a violent fit of temper on the slightest provocation. I had a distinct impression that some burden of trouble lay heavy upon his mind; he did indeed confess, at one moment, that business was bad, and that he was worried about his investments, but I attached little importance to this, for the Greene family were all so immensely rich that I found it impossible to imagine any of them being seriously inconvenienced by even a temporary lack of funds.

The weather was bleak, with frequent and drenching downpours of rain, so that even Geoffrey was forced to remain, for the greater part of the day, indoors. This not unnaturally increased the friction between himself and Madge, and as though this were not enough, a series of minor domestic misfortunes supervened. The eldest child, Tony, developed a bad cold, which seemed likely to "go to his chest", and Madge insisted upon calling in the doctor, which Geoffrey condemned as an extravagance (it was noteworthy that he seemed, nowadays, to have become infected with Madge's habitual stinginess). The fish for Saturday night's dinner didn't arrive, and there was chaos in the kitchen; Madge had forgotten to order coffee; one of the dogs—a newly-acquired Sealyham puppy—made a mess in Geoffrey's dressing-room, and since the dog belonged to Madge, she was held responsible.

On Sunday morning we drove Madge to church, and afterwards went for a drink to the King's Arms; but Geoffrey, even after three or four pints of beer, remained as morose and preoccupied as ever. In the afternoon the rain set in with a relentless persistence, and our nerves became increasingly frayed. Tony was not so well, the newsagent had sent the *People* instead of the *Sunday Times*, the fire wouldn't burn because the logs were damp ("I *did* ask you to make sure they were brought in in good time," Madge shrilly protested to Geoffrey).

Things reached a climax at tea-time, when a party of Greene cousins turned up, all of them very jolly after a luncheon-party in Sevenoaks, smoking cigars and roaring with laughter at their own jokes. They had, as it turned out, invited themselves a week before, but Madge had clean forgotten, and the tea-table, when they arrived, was only too obviously laid for ourselves alone. The cousins proceeded to chaff Geoffrey, rather disobligingly, about some matter of business, and he lost his temper; Madge did her best to restore peace, but her shrill chatter was becoming more and more hysterical, and I had an unpleasant feeling that she might, at any moment, burst into tears.

The cousins left at last, and no sooner had they gone, than Geoffrey, still in a filthy temper, stumped out to the dining-room, reappearing a minute later with a large tumbler of whisky in his hand.

"Help yourselves if you want some," he barked at us, in a tone so malevolent that one might have supposed him to have laced the whisky-bottle with cyanide. "*You'd* better keep off it though," he added, with a gratuitous unkindness, to Nigel.

Geoffrey drank whisky solidly till dinner-time, watched with barely-concealed fury by Madge, who had pointedly refused a drink herself, though she must have longed for one. I had never known Geoffrey do such a thing before, and I began to feel rather frightened. After dinner, however, he was sufficiently mellowed to propose some game with a board and counters, for which he had lately had a mild craze. Nigel, still in a bad temper, refused to play, though he insisted upon standing by the table and watching the game with an irritating air of condescension. I myself played with great stupidity, and more than once Geoffrey snapped at me rudely. As for poor Madge, her forced air of brightness became more painfully brittle as the evening wore on; to do her justice, however, she did behave with great tact and self-possession, and I couldn't help feeling sorry for her.

It was Geoffrey's turn to throw. At that moment, Madge turned away from the table to admonish the Sealyham, who had jumped on to a forbidden chair. I got up to remove the dog, and just as I did so heard the clatter of the dice upon the board and Geoffrey's voice saying, with brisk satisfaction, "Jolly old six to me". A moment before, Nigel had moved away from the table to peer at the bookshelf in the corner; now I saw that he had returned and was standing directly behind his brother, looking down at the board. Geoffrey had already picked up the dice, but too late: I heard Nigel give an indignant gasp.

"But it wasn't a six, it was a two!" he exclaimed.

Geoffrey, suddenly aware of Nigel's presence at his back, swivelled round abruptly in his chair.

"What's that?" he said sharply.

Nigel turned to Madge and myself, with that air of half-frightened defiance which I knew so well.

"It's perfectly true," he said. "Geoff called a six, and it was only a two. I was standing behind him, and I saw it."

"Nonsense," spluttered Geoffrey, "of course it was a six."

"It wasn't a six, and you know it," Nigel retorted.

Geoffrey had jumped to his feet and turned upon Nigel, his face blazing with indignation.

"Good God, man, are you accusing me of cheating?" he shouted, taking a step forward. For a moment I really thought he was going to strike his brother; Nigel evidently thought so too, for he stumbled backwards, clumsily, upsetting a reading-lamp from Madge's worktable and smashing the bulb.

"Oh, Nigel, *really*!" screamed Madge, to whom, perhaps, the damaged lamp seemed of greater moment than Nigel's aspersions upon her husband's honour.

"I ask you," stormed Geoffrey, "do you accuse me of cheating? Answer me, yes or no!"

I looked at Nigel, expecting that he would repeat his accusation. But Geoffrey's thunderous outburst, the smashed lamp, Madge's screams, had been too much for him; his self-confidence suddenly collapsed, and with a shrug of his shoulders he turned sullenly away.

"Will you or will you not answer my question?" Geoffrey snapped at him.

"Well, it *looked* like a two, to me," Nigel feebly replied.

"A mistake, obviously," Madge cut in, with tact. She was on her knees, trying to extricate the lamp from a tangle of flex.

"Look here, my lad, either you're telling me I cheated, or you're not," Geoffrey insisted. For all his bluster, there was, I thought, a shifty, almost a frightened look in his eye.

"Oh for goodness' sake stop quarrelling, you two," exclaimed Madge, with an attempt at a laugh. "It's only a game, after all, and I expect Nigel made a mistake, or else Geoff did—he's getting frightfully short-sighted, I keep telling him to go to an oculist, but I might as well talk to a brick wall. Nigel, just ring the bell, will you, and we'll get Minnie to sweep up the broken glass. Geoff, darling, do hold on to the lamp-stand while I unwind this beastly wire."

It was not long before Madge had things firmly in hand, and by the time the lamp had been salvaged and a new bulb fitted, peace of a kind was restored. Nobody, however, felt much like resuming the game, and the rest of the evening was passed in an atmosphere of tension which even Madge's tactful behaviour could not wholly disperse; Tranby Croft itself, I thought, could scarcely have been less cosy. Soon Geoffrey brought out the whisky again, and this time Madge did accept a drink, making it the occasion for a somewhat hysterical though well-meant outburst of gaiety.

"Cheers!" she said. "I'm sure we all needed a peggy-weg."

She sipped her own very *chota* peggy-weg extremely slowly, and Geoffrey shortly got up to refill his own glass.

"Geoff, dear," she exclaimed, "do be an angel and take Musso out for his walkie." (Musso was the new Sealyham.) Then, turning to me, she began to discuss with great animation the new Book Society choice, which rather unfortunately I had not read. When Geoffrey had departed, unwillingly, with Musso, she broke off to address her brother-in-law.

"Nigel, my dear, just take the whisky back to the dining-room, would you? I expect Minnie's gone to bed, and we shan't want any more."

"Geoff will, probably," Nigel said meaningly.

"Well, if he does, he can always go and get it," Madge retorted rather tartly. "I do hate seeing bottles and glasses littering the room, it looks so sordid."

Geoffrey, returning ten minutes later, saw that the bottle had gone, and sent Nigel to fetch it. With a defiant glance at Madge, he poured out nearly half a tumblerful for himself and a smaller quantity for me. By bedtime—for the first time since I had known him—he was noticeably the worse for liquor. Madge, very wisely, said nothing, but her looks spoke volumes; nor were these (I thought) of the kind which is commonly chosen by the Book Society.

My bedroom, as it happened, was next to that of Geoffrey and Madge; the intervening wall was not very thick, and they had probably forgotten where I was sleeping. For half an hour or so after I had gone to bed, I heard their voices raised in a lengthy and acrimonious argument, punctuated by occasional thumps as Geoffrey—who was far from steady on his legs—stumbled about the room. At one point, Madge's voice rose almost to a scream, following a particularly loud bang, and I wondered if Geoffrey had struck her.

At last the voices ceased, and I heard Geoffrey retire to the small dressing-room on the farther side of the bedroom in which he slept (he had preferred, so I gathered, to sleep alone for some years now, partly from a dislike of feminine fripperies, but chiefly in order that he might lie with his head immediately below a wide-open window). After his door had finally banged, there was silence for some time; then, as I lay reading, I heard the muffled sound of sobs coming from the next room. The noise continued for what seemed a long time; I tried not to listen, forcing myself to concentrate upon a novel by Charles Morgan. I was not especially fond of Madge, but I was easily moved to pity, and to hear her thus desolately weeping in the darkness distressed me very much. She was not, perhaps, the sort of person whom one most easily associates with pathos; yet I now found myself thinking with, sudden compassion, of all the small things which made up her life, and which I was accustomed, with a callow superciliousness, to despise: her dogs, her Book Society choices, her treasured ornaments, the prints of flying geese. Poor Madge, I thought, had tried hard to make the best of a bad job; she did, it was true, nag at her husband, but Geoffrey, after all, would have provoked the most placid of women into some sort of protest. Even her parsimony, I felt, could to some extent be excused: the Greenes, though rich, were extravagant, and Madge, if she tended to be rather off-hand in her maternal rôle, had a strong sense of duty towards her children. She ought, I reflected, to have married some nice young man in the Buffs, as poor as herself; instead, she had married into the Greene clan—a fate for which she was no better fitted than her mother-in-law, who also, perhaps, in the past, had lain sobbing in the darkness as poor Madge was sobbing now.

CHAPTER FIVE

A Spot of Trouble

Early in the following year it was decided that I should be given a job in my father's business at Folkestone. This experiment was obviously doomed to failure, for I was congenitally hopeless at figures, and loathed working in an office; nonetheless, I was glad enough in many ways to leave London, and on the whole rather enjoyed this latest (and, as it proved, last) attempt on my part to come to terms with the Reality Principle.

I had heard nothing of the Greenes for some time, and indeed had hardly, since I left London, given them a thought; my friendship with Nigel was not of the kind which engenders correspondence, and on my rare visits to Blackheath I made no effort to seek him out. Nor was I again invited to Four Winds, and if I had been, I think I should have refused the invitation, for my last week-end there had virtually cured me of my romantic infatuation for Philistia. There were rumours—which reached me through my brother—that the estrangement of Geoffrey and Madge had entered upon a new and more acute phase: it was even said that Geoffrey wanted a divorce.

"If you ask me, there's something rather odd going on in that quarter," said my brother, with a certain wicked relish. "I saw Geoff at the club the other night" (both Geoffrey and my brother belonged to the Senior), "and he seems to have gone all to pieces. He was drinking like a fish, and kept on saying he was 'ruined'. Of course, that's all nonsense—why, ——and Co." (he named Geoffrey's firm) "are as safe as houses, and in any case the Greenes are all stinking with money."

It was not long after this that the appalling, the incredible news burst upon us. I heard it first from my brother, who had just returned, on the Sunday night, from Blackheath.

"I suppose you've not *heard*?" he said, in a tone of such horrific excitement that I positively felt myself shiver.

"Heard what?" I gasped, imagining floods and holocausts, financial ruin, my parents murdered in their beds.

"About Geoffrey—Geoffrey Greene?" said my brother, with a maddening deliberation.

"Of course I haven't heard," I said impatiently. "What on earth's happened to Geoffrey?"

My brother paused for several seconds, extracting—as was his habit—the last ounce of drama from the situation.

"He's been arrested," he said at last.

"*Arrested?*" I echoed, in a tone so genuinely flabbergasted as to satisfy even my brother's taste for the dramatic. "What on earth for?" It must at the very least, I thought, be rape or manslaughter, if not murder.

My brother paused for another instant, then, almost in a whisper, muttered the single monosyllable:

"Fraud."

The mean, squalid little word seemed to taint the air like a bad smell. Rape or murder would have seemed less degrading, more consonant with Geoffrey's dignity. I asked for details, but about these my brother was rather vague; nor, for that matter, was I ever absolutely certain as to the exact nature of the charges brought against Geoffrey. There was, I think, some question of the maladministration of a trust-fund, in some way connected with his business; he was also charged with a more direct and flagrant misappropriation of the firm's money, and of falsifying the accounts. The whole affair was extremely complex, and since I was notably ignorant in financial matters, I found the facts difficult to grasp.

Geoffrey was at present out on bail; he would not come up for trial for some weeks. The news had been brought to my family by poor Molly, who had naturally been anxious that they should hear it from her before it appeared in the newspapers. My father had been particularly shocked: according to my brother, he had at first refused to believe it. "I never liked the chap," he was reported to have said, "but at least I thought he was *straight*."

My brother was of the same opinion; as for myself, though I, too, was shocked by the news, I couldn't pretend that I found it very surprising.

A few days later we heard that old Herbert Greene had had a slight stroke: nothing very serious, he was not paralysed, and it was said that, if he took things carefully, he would in all likelihood make a complete recovery. There was no doubt, however, in anybody's mind, about the cause of the attack; and we were all agreed that it made things very much harder for poor Geoffrey.

About this time I spent a week-end in London. On the Saturday night I dined with a friend at Bertorelli's, in Charlotte Street, and afterwards went for a drink to the Fitzroy. Here I was immediately confronted by Nigel, more than half drunk, and conducting a lively conversation with Nina Hamnett.

"I suppose you've heard about Geoff?" he said excitedly.

I said I had.

"Serve him bloody well right," Nigel said, viciously. "He's always been a twister."

"But he may be perfectly innocent," I protested.

"Not on your bloody life," Nigel retorted, and gave one of his shrill little giggles.

I didn't feel overmuch sympathy for Geoffrey myself, but Nigel's attitude struck me as both shocking and repellent. He was quite obviously gloating over his brother's downfall, and seemed totally oblivious of the suffering which it must bring to the rest of the family; even his father's illness appeared to strike him as comical rather than otherwise.

"How about Madge?" I asked.

"Oh, she's being the gallant little woman, just as you'd expect— clenching her teeth and being terrifically loyal, you know." Nigel grinned at me nastily, and I noticed that his own teeth, never very good ones, were badly discoloured by caries.

Here Nina interrupted to suggest that I bought her a drink, and having done so, I made my escape.

Next morning I ran into Nigel again, at the Three Tuns; he had a bad hangover, but was still inclined to take a jaunty and cynical line about his brother. In fact, as I could guess, Geoffrey's misfortune had affected him more than he cared to admit: Geoffrey, after all, had been held up to him, throughout his life, as a model of probity and rectitude; for Nigel he had been, at least in earlier days, a hero, and that this god-like figure should have turned out to have feet of clay must have come as something of a shock.

Changing the subject, I asked Nigel about his painting.

"Oh, I'm slogging along, you know. I've rather an idea I might have a small exhibition soon. There's a chap at the Wertheimer Gallery—in Bloomsbury, you know—who's rather interested in my work. I feel I'm about through with the Goldsmith—they're really hopelessly academic, I think I've learnt about all they can teach me, and Frankie thinks the same. I saw her the other day, by the way—she was asking after you."

I asked Nigel about his mother, whom I hadn't seen for some time.

"Oh, she's going dotty," he said. "There's madness in her family, you know—her aunt Cecilia had to go into a loony-bin, and all her children were a bit touched, too."

I asked how Mrs. Greene had taken the news about Geoffrey.

"Oh, she swears he's innocent, of course: she thinks Geoff's partner's to blame, because he came to dinner once and got tight, and was rude to the pater. I must say he's a frightfully common little man."

As though they had not misfortunes enough, the Greenes were now prostrated by a further disaster. This was occasioned by Oonagh, who chose this inopportune moment to announce the staggering news that she was engaged to be married. Her fiancé was a little man called Greengrass, a clerk in Nigel's insurance office; Oonagh, it seemed, had met him at the annual staff dance

105

of the company, and they had been walking out, in a dim and furtive way, ever since.

There was really nothing against Mr. Greengrass, except that he was poor, had a Cockney accent and looked rather like a mouse. Oonagh's engagement, however, created an appalling rumpus: that she should wish to marry an insurance clerk earning three pounds a week, seemed to the Greenes almost more degrading than Geoffrey's impending trial for fraudulent conversion. At first, the news was kept from old Mr. Greene, to whom, it was felt, this new shock might easily prove fatal. Oonagh, however, had no such scruples, and finally settled the matter by marching into her father's room, when no one was looking, and telling him herself.

Mr. Greene, as it happened, was not struck dead by this thunderbolt; on the contrary, its effect was rather beneficial than otherwise, stimulating his mental faculties to such a degree that within a week of hearing the news he was well on the way to recovery. At first, it is true, he was perfectly furious, and declared his intention of cutting Oonagh out of his will; but Oonagh, after all, was already in her mid-thirties, and must be credited with knowing her own mind. Her lover was perfectly respectable, and if she insisted on marrying a little man like a mouse, no power on earth could stop her. Such were the stark facts, and Mr. Greene, having faced them, at last surrendered with a fairly good grace.

They were married, very quietly (in striking contrast to the usual practice among the Greenes) a couple of months later. A reasonable income had been settled upon Oonagh, and by adding a proportion of her money to his own savings, Mr. Greengrass was enabled to realize his life's ambition, and buy a small farm in Essex. There he and Oonagh prospered, in a modest way, and though childless the marriage was apparently a perfectly happy one.

The Greenes, however, could never really bring themselves to forgive Oonagh; she, for her part, proceeded to cut herself off almost completely from her family, and in the ensuing months her name was scarcely ever mentioned at The Grange.

I saw Geoffrey only once during the period before his trial, meeting him casually in the street, one Sunday, at Blackheath. He looked haggard and a good deal older, but had obviously decided to brazen things out.

"You heard about my spot of trouble, I suppose?" he said to me, in his usual jaunty tone. "Of course, the whole thing's a put-up job: the fact is, I'm the junior partner and they're making a scapegoat of me. I've told them a few home-truths in my time, and of course they don't like me any the more for it."

Geoffrey, I had gathered from other sources, was seeking the best legal advice, and seemed fairly confident about the outcome of the trial. It was some years before I was to see him again; meanwhile, I remained at Folkestone, and such news as I received of the Greenes was at second or third hand.

Geoffrey came up for trial about two or three weeks after my last meeting with him. It was a long and complex case, and many of the financial dealings involved were beyond my comprehension. Much of the evidence seemed, circumstantially, extremely damning, and I had little doubt in my own mind that Geoffrey would be found guilty. In the end, he was acquitted on all charges: certain of the evidence was deemed insufficient, but his acquittal appeared to be mainly due to the scoring of a number of purely technical points by his defending lawyer. There was much discussion as to whether he had connived at or merely, from ignorance, condoned certain actions on the part of his colleagues; what finally emerged, at the end of the case, was that Geoffrey's conduct in the various transactions involved had been just—but only just—within the limits of the law. In the summing-up it was hinted—and indeed more than hinted—that he had been morally if not legally culpable, and the damning phrase "sharp practice" was used more than once.

This would have been bad enough, but the case for the prosecution involved a good deal of probing into Geoffrey's private affairs. His financial position was found to be extremely unstable: for some years he had been living almost entirely on credit, and a series of substantial monthly payments to a certain Mrs. van Houten, of Belsize Park, was called into question. This lady turned out to be

Geoffrey's mistress; there were other items of expenditure, too, all of which pointed to his increasing irresponsibility in money matters. It was hardly surprising, I thought, that, during my last visit to Four Winds, he should have been unwilling to run up unnecessary household bills.

Geoffrey, of course, resigned his directorship of the firm; he also, as I heard from my brother, resigned from his club. It was understood that he would like Madge to divorce him—there being now abundant grounds for such a proceeding—but that she had refused to do so, on account of the children. Meanwhile, Four Winds was put up for sale, and during the weeks following the trial Madge and the children stayed at The Grange, while Geoffrey took himself off on a sailing trip up the Essex coast.

My brother happened to meet Madge at this time, during a week-end at Blackheath, and from what he told me I gathered that she was being, as Nigel had satirically remarked on an earlier occasion, "terrifically loyal". This I could easily believe, and was not, like Nigel, tempted to sneer at the way in which she was coping with her difficult situation. Madge, I thought, had her good qualities: she was not, for instance, particularly fond of children, but she was obviously prepared to make sacrifices for her own offspring. I remembered my last week-end at Four Winds, lying in bed and listening to her hopeless sobbing in the darkness; thinking of that night, I felt my pity for her revive, and felt saddened by the thought of her having to leave her "jolly" house, to which, I think, she had been genuinely attached.

Geoffrey, she had told my brother, was thinking of going in for chicken-farming: he had heard of a nice little place near Princes Risborough which, apparently, was going cheap. The house was hardly more than a bungalow, but the country was pretty, and it would be nice for the children.

At The Grange—so I heard from my mother, who felt impelled to visit poor Molly, if only to show that Geoffrey's disgrace had made no "difference"—the atmosphere could not have been more gloomy if Geoffrey had been convicted and sent to gaol. Old Mr.

Greene who, whatever his other weaknesses, was entirely upright and scrupulous in financial matters, had been horrified that any son of his should be even suspected of dishonourable conduct, and the verdict itself had done little to console him.

As for Molly, she seemed, said my mother, to have grown twenty years older. She still refused to believe that Geoffrey was even morally guilty, but the fact remained that his name had been "dragged through the courts", and to Molly's intensely respectable soul this was a disaster from which, as she confessed, she didn't think she could ever recover. Her only comfort at this time was Madge who, during her stay at The Grange, treated her with great kindness; also, she much enjoyed spoiling her grandchildren, for whom she developed a fondness which, perhaps, exceeded any that she had ever felt for her own rather graceless brood.

A year passed, during which Geoffrey's "spot of trouble" began gradually to be forgotten. He and Madge had settled down, after a fashion, at Princes Risborough, and the chicken-farm promised to do reasonably well. As for Nigel, he continued to attend the Goldsmith School, though complaining bitterly of the "academic" prejudices of his instructors. I saw little of him during this time, being mainly out of London, but I gathered that he spent many of his evenings in Fitzrovia; his health had apparently improved, though he was still subject to periodical relapses. On the few occasions when I encountered him he struck me as being dirtier and in general more careless about himself than ever; once I asked him about the exhibition which he had been going to have at the Wertheimer Gallery, but this, he said, had been indefinitely postponed.

CHAPTER SIX

The House in Ruins

Old Mr. Greene died in the late summer of 1934. He had never really recovered, it seemed, from the shock occasioned by Geoffrey's misconduct; he had not had another stroke, but had become gradually weaker and weaker, finally expiring after an attack of pneumonia. Apart from a transient and rather sentimental pity for Molly, I couldn't pretend that the news meant much to me. Such interest as I had once felt in the Greenes had long since subsided: I had written off Nigel as bogus and a bore; as for Geoffrey and Madge, I remembered my *culte* for them with the kind of embarrassment with which one recalls the more callow indiscretions of one's adolescence.

I heard in due course that the old man's fortune had turned out to be a good deal smaller than had been expected; he had apparently indulged in some unfortunate speculations during his later years, and also left a number of annuities to persons of the female sex whose claims upon him did not bear too close an examination. His estate, even so, proved to be of sufficiently respectable dimensions; the bulk of it was left in trust to Molly for her lifetime, and after her death would be divided between the three children or their descendants. A certain proportion, apart from the trust-fund, had been made over to Geoffrey and Nigel; I do not know to what extent Geoffrey benefited, but Nigel, apparently, came in for about £250 a year, with the prospect, of course, of a share in the remaining capital on the death of his mother.

Shortly after Mr. Greene's death, The Grange was sold up: poor Molly had taken a dislike to the house, and could hardly, for that matter, have afforded its upkeep. She decided, after much diffuse and inconsequent meditation, to take a flat at Bournemouth, where several of her Tufnell relations were established, including two eccentric female cousins, daughters of her mad Aunt Cecilia.

Molly herself could not bear to be present at the sale; my mother, however, did attend the auction of "household effects", and bought a garden seat, two Bohemian glass vases and a china cat. The sale, on the whole, realized a satisfactory sum, though the French pictures were knocked down—as I had rather expected they would be—for a derisory figure.

The house itself was bought by a rich speculative builder in Lewisham, who converted it into what he called "luxury flats". The speculation was not a great success: during the next five years the flats were occupied by a succession of tenants, none of whom stayed very long; the house was too cold, too far from the station, and people complained that it was "gloomy". During the war, it received a direct hit from a land-mine; today the site is occupied by a block of very functional working-class flats, for which, however, the house's original name has been retained—with a very proper feeling for historic continuity—by the local council.

I had now lost touch with Nigel almost completely. Occasionally, on my rare forays into Fitzrovia, I would encounter Frankie, who by now had become very socially conscious and left-wing. What she really liked (I gathered) about the Popular Front was the endless opportunities it gave her for rescuing people: the increasing stream of refugees was obviously right up her street. Once I went to a party in Acacia Road; Frankie's bookshelves, which had once held an interesting collection of "modern firsts"—Huxley, Lawrence, Virginia Woolf—were now filled with the publications of the Left Book Club and various Faber poets (it was rumoured that Wystan Auden had once been present, for a few minutes, at one of her parties).

I asked her if she still saw anything of Nigel Greene.

"Oh yes, he's thinking of having a show of his pictures," she said. "He's a terribly unhappy person, it might cheer him up."

Not long after this—it was the summer of 1936—I received an

invitation to a private view at the Wertheimer Gallery in Bloomsbury: "Paintings and Drawings by Nigel Tufnell-Greene."

So Nigel, I thought, had achieved his ambition at last; and, being in London at the time, I went to the show.

I arrived at the gallery about midday; only one or two people, besides myself, were present, and these looked, I thought, like critics. Suddenly, from an inner room, a tall man with a beard, dressed in a corduroy suit and a very eccentric tie, sidled rather nervously into the gallery and greeted me by name. With a start of surprise—and only after several moments' delay—I recognized Nigel.

I was quite shocked by his appearance: it was not merely the beard and the clothes which had effected the change in him; he looked broken down, ill and—despite his air of nervous excitement—unhappy. Several of his teeth were missing, and those which remained obviously needed extracting; his hair, as untidy and dirty-looking as ever, was beginning to recede from his forehead. He looked about forty, though he couldn't, in fact, have been more than twenty-nine.

He greeted me with his old air of shy defiance; obviously he was thrilled by the exhibition, yet just as plainly he was tortured by an intense anxiety.

"So glad you could come, do excuse me, I must just see Billy Wertheimer for a second, come and have a drink afterwards," he gasped at me, all in one breath. He vanished into the office, and I was left—much to my relief—to examine the pictures in solitude.

I don't know what I had expected: I had seen nothing of Nigel's work since he went to the art school, but my memories of his pathetic daubs, exhibited so self-consciously in the attic at The Grange, didn't encourage me to hope for anything very brilliant. The paintings now on view were, as it happened, just about what one might have inferred from Nigel's early efforts, taking into consideration his years at the Goldsmith School. In subject they differed little from the canvases which I remembered: most of them had title like "Soldiers fighting in a bar", "Death of a child", "Street accident", "All-in Wrestlers", and so forth. The drawing had hardly improved at all, and the paint still had the same dense, palette-knife texture; but Nigel, despite his contempt for the Goldsmith School, had certainly acquired a trick or two. He had managed, for instance, in some way to stylize his figures, so that they looked less obviously out of drawing; probably he had looked at the work of Edward Burra, and perhaps William Roberts as well. His slightly cubist distortions were at least consciously contrived, and not, as formerly, the result of a mere congenital inability to draw. I thought the paintings very bad, but there was a violent, flashy quality about some of them which might impress certain critics of the less exacting type.

I had a drink with Nigel later in the Museum Tavern, just round the corner. Fortunately he was much too excited by his show to worry about my own reactions to the pictures, and I was not required—as I had feared I might be—to give my considered opinion of their merits. I did say that I thought his painting had much improved, which in a sense was perfectly true; for the rest, I contented myself by saying that I hoped he would make lots of money, though really I thought this highly unlikely.

I asked for news of Geoffrey and Madge. The chicken-farm, it appeared, was not doing so well as had been expected; Nigel had spent one or two week-ends there, and from his account of it, Dunroamin (which, regrettably, was the name of the house) sounded anything but cosy.

"It's really incredibly depressing," said Nigel. "An awful bungaloid affair, right on the main road. They both work like niggers, they never go out, and hardly know a soul. Madge wants to start breeding silver foxes, but they don't think they can raise the capital. They're sending Tony to some very posh prep, school next term, and that's going to make a hole in their income. And then, of course, Geoff's drinking like a fish nowadays."

I asked Nigel where he himself was living.

"Oh, I've got a small flat in Howland Street," he told me. "I share it with a Friend," he added, contriving to invest the harmless monosyllable with a quality both sacred and slightly sinister. Given the address, I had visions of a *drôle de ménage* in the manner of

Verlaine and Rimbaud, though Nigel, I felt, was singularly ill-equipped to fill either of these exacting rôles.

"I hope you don't fling rotten herrings at his head," I remarked, with a misplaced facetiousness.

"*Herrings?*" queried Nigel, in bewilderment. Obviously he hadn't caught the allusion, and I couldn't be bothered to explain it. A few minutes later I had to hurry away to an appointment. Before I left, Nigel gave me his address, and I agreed to look him up, sometime, in Howland Street; though to tell the truth I had no very firm intention of fulfilling my promise.

Nigel's exhibition, so I gathered from the notices which I read of it, must have fallen as flat as a pancake. It wasn't so much that the critics damned it: they just didn't, for the most part, deign to notice it at all. The few who did confined their comments to a short non-committal paragraph at the end of some article on "Current Exhibitions"; the sole exception was the critic of one of the more influential left-wing weeklies, who wrote a long and glowing review in which he hailed Mr. Tufnell-Greene as an apostle of "socialist realism". The street accidents, the scenes of flogging and fighting which supplied most of Nigel's subjects, were interpreted in strictly Marxist terms as episodes in the class-struggle; of the paintings themselves—considered purely as paintings—the writer said little, merely remarking, in an apologetic aside, that he found their *impasto* a trifle too "striated" for his taste.

I wondered what Nigel thought of this review; no doubt it had delighted him, though he must, I thought, have been mildly surprised—and perhaps not altogether gratified—at finding himself thus dragooned into the Marxist fold. The only other reference to the show which came my way, and which seems worthy of note, was a short paragraph in the *Daily Express* gossip-column, in which Mr. William Hickey informed his readers that one of Nigel's more ferocious pictures, depicting a convict being flogged, had been bought by a well-known dramatic critic. Knowing something, by hearsay, of this gentleman's somewhat eccentric love-life, I couldn't feel that his purchase was really much of a compliment to Nigel.

It must have been about six months after Nigel's show that, finding myself once again in the neighbourhood of Charlotte Street, I went into the Fitzroy for a drink. The first person I saw was Nigel: it was a moment or two before I recognized him, for he wore a pair of horn-rimmed spectacles; his sight, I thought, must have become worse, for in the past he had avoided, so far as possible, wearing his glasses in public. His clothes, too, had undergone a significant change: in place of the arty corduroys and flowing tie, he now wore a pair of workman's canvas trousers and a rather grubby flannel shirt, open at the neck.

"Hullo, mate," he greeted me, with a slight Cockney accent.

One would normally have supposed that both the accent and the form of address were intended to be funny or ironic, yet Nigel's expression was perfectly serious, and I noticed, moreover, that he retained the Cockney twang in speaking to the barman. He carried a basket containing several quart bottles of pale ale and a volume from the Left Book Club called *Whither the Left?*

It was apparent that Nigel had obeyed the call of the *Zeitgeist* and become a Communist.

When I had bought him a drink, he explained that he was just going back to his flat, and asked me to come too. I had no particular engagements, and agreed to accompany him. He seemed rather restive, and a minute or two later suggested making a move: Reg, he added, was expecting him. This I presumed to be the Friend of whom Nigel had spoken at our last meeting, and I felt curious to see what kind of soul-mate he had chosen for himself.

The flat proved to be a basement one, dark, gloomy and extremely squalid. There was a minimum of furniture, and the walls were hung with Nigel's pictures, most of which I recognized from the exhibition; I concluded—rightly, as it happened—that very few had been sold. On the table were various unwashed plates, knives and forks, and one or two empty sardine tins; a small bookshelf harboured other volumes published by the Left Book Club. There

115

was a film of dust over everything, and a peculiar smell compounded of stale food, bad drains and escaping gas.

As we entered the sitting-room, I observed a person whom I took to be some visiting workman—a plumber or a gas-fitter, perhaps. This, however, proved to be Reg. He ignored me completely, and, taking a look at the basket which Nigel carried, exclaimed: "Christ, you silly bastard, you've forgotten the gin."

I saw Nigel flinch, and a frightened look come into his eyes.

"Sorry, I'd run out of cash," he apologized.

"Ballocks to that, you could have cashed a cheque with old Kleinfeld, couldn't you?"

"I can't actually, till Friday—it would probably bounce."

"Oh well, for Christ's sake get some glasses and let's have some wallop."

Nigel obeyed, and I was at last, belatedly, introduced to Reg. He gave me an insolent grin, and said:

"I suppose you're one of Bert's highbrow friends, aren't you?"

"Bert?" I said, bewildered.

"Oh, Reg calls me Bert," Nigel explained rapidly. "After all, it is my name in a way—I mean, my middle name's Herbert, you see, and I hate being called Nigel, it sounds so frightfully bourgeois."

The way Nigel pronounced this word, in a French accent, but with a marked Cockney twang, was highly instructive. Having produced the three tumblers, he hesitated, peering at the one which he held in his hand: I could see that it was grubby, with bits of fluff adhering to its sides.

"I'd better just rinse them out, I think", he said nervously, and was moving towards the kitchen when Reg gave a contemptuous laugh.

"Gertcher," he exclaimed, "you and your upper-class prejudices. The beer won't taste no different just for a bit of dust."

So we drank beer out of the dirty glasses.

I don't know quite what I had expected of Reg, but I had, I suppose, vaguely imagined him as somebody young and fairly personable. The reality came as a shock, for Reg was hideous, and must have been at least forty, if not more. He had the figure of a heavyweight boxer, slightly run to seed, and a bloated face which reminded me of a decomposing melon. A shock of black, greasy hair dangled over his forehead, his teeth were filthy, so were his nails; he wore a very tight pair of canvas trousers and a grey, collarless shirt gaping open to his waist. He spoke with a strong Cockney accent, though with occasional traces of an acquired suburban gentility.

I was appalled by this horrible creature, and wondered how on earth Nigel could have taken up with him. That Nigel possessed a streak of masochism was probable enough, but it seemed to me flatly incredible that anybody, however *outré* his tastes, should really find Reg attractive or even tolerable. It was obvious, moreover, that Nigel was terrified of him: at every movement of Reg, every remark that he uttered, I saw him wince like a frightened puppy. I tried to talk to him about his painting: when was he going to have another show? Nigel, however, seemed unwilling to discuss the matter, and our conversation was inhibited still further by the exasperating behaviour of Reg, who kept up an intermittent monologue, addressed to nobody in particular, and consisting in the main of pseudo-political slogans and Cockney-Army catchwords: "Up the workers", "Roll-on-Christmas-and-let's-have-some-nuts", "Mother's drunk again", etc., etc.

I was excruciatingly bored, and the squalid room, plastered with Nigel's unsold pictures, induced in me a profound depression. Why had Nigel chosen to live in this den, I wondered? It was not as though he were really so poor: in those days one could live decently if not luxuriously on £250 a year. Perhaps Nigel was being blackmailed by Reg; but more probably, I thought, his reasons for this curious form of self-torture were, in the main, ideological.

At last I could stick it no longer, and made an excuse to go. Nigel, looking at his watch, replied that he must be going too.

"Actually, I've got to go to a meeting," he said, adding, in a hushed and pious tone: "About Spain, you know." He turned to Reg, with an air half-pleading, half-apprehensive. "I suppose you're not coming, are you?"

Reg let out a crude guffaw.

"Not on your bloody life," he said, and poured out some more beer for himself. He turned to me with a wolfish grin. "I wonder he don't go and fight for the bastards, if he's so bleedin' worried about 'em. Eh, Bert, me old cock-sparrow?"

Nigel gave a nervous, shamefaced laugh, and we left the flat together. He was catching a tube-train at Goodge Street, and I walked with him as far as the station. He explained to me the nature of the meeting for which he was bound, adding that, but for his health, he would have already joined the International Brigade. Unfortunately, as he explained, he was still obliged to have periodic courses of prostatic massage, which might not be easy to arrange in Spain. He proceeded to lecture me, for the length of our walk, about the necessity for Taking Sides, Throwing in One's Lot with the Proletariat and supporting the Fight against Fascism (which he pronounced, curiously, *fascisme*, as though it were a word not of Italian but of French origin). His arguments were banal in the extreme: I had read them all, over and over again, in the left-wing magazines and pamphlets which flourished at that time; even to me, who had no pretensions to be politically-minded, Nigel's homily seemed muddle-headed and singularly ill-informed. I realized, all the same, that it must be nice for him to have found a cause which so conveniently justified his innate rebelliousness and his natural tendency to be dirty and untidy.

Arrived at the station, Nigel turned to me and asked me the question which I had been dreading: what did I think of Reg?

I said I expected he was very agreeable, but that I didn't really know him well enough to judge.

Nigel gave me a look which could only be described as starry-eyed—in striking contrast with his habitual expression when in the presence of Reg himself.

"He's really a *wonderful* person, when you get to know him," he assured me. "He's so absolutely *natural*, you see. Of course, his parents were Real Working Class, which is such an enormous advantage, don't you think? Reg is really a Child of Nature, he lives a genuinely *instinctual* life, if you see what I mean—" (Nigel brought out this impressive word with a rather self-conscious emphasis, as though he had just picked it up) "—and he thinks with his solar plexus, so to speak, not with his brain."

I said that I could quite believe this, and that it must be very nice; though it was odd, I thought, how Marxists seemed able to absorb the dottier ideas of D. H. Lawrence with such apparent ease, and without a trace of mental indigestion.

Later that same evening I ran across Nina Hamnett in the Marquis of Granby, and from her learnt a few salient facts about Nigel's "Child of Nature".

"Wonderful torso, my dear, just like a Greco-Roman gladiator. Nigel's thrilled to death, of course, he's got plenty of mon, can't paint for nuts, but he's a sweetie, and I adore him."

I learnt further that Reg had been a familiar figure about Charlotte Street for the last year or so; he described himself, for convenience, as an artists' model, though his earnings from this source amounted to little more than a few half-crowns a week if he was lucky. His earlier career had apparently been passed in the Army; since then he had been in turn a professional prize-fighter, a racing tout, a porter at Covent Garden market and an amateur cracksman—which latter activity had procured him the unaccustomed luxury of a six-months' sojourn in one of His Majesty's prisons.

"Nigel says he thinks with his solar plexus," I said to Nina.

"You bet he does," she replied emphatically. "And my God, *what* a solar plexus, too."

Nigel's conversion to Communism was hardly surprising, for this, after all, was 1937, and for people like Nigel, at that period, Communism had all the seductive glamour which the Church of Rome had exerted, a hundred years before, upon similarly unstable characters. I was not unsympathetic; in a sense, indeed, I rather envied him, though I was far from envying his present way of life. Nor, with the best will in the world, could I take his Communism very seriously: I was particularly amused by his solemn attempts to assume a Cockney accent, at which he was notably unsuccessful, though really, I thought—with what, I fear, was a touch of snobbery—such an accomplishment should not have presented any great difficulty to a son of old Herbert Greene.

It so happened that, during the next few weeks, I tended for various reasons, social or amorous, which need not be specified, to frequent the pubs and restaurants of Fitzrovia. I met Nigel on a number of occasions, and once or twice revisited the flat in Howland Street. Nigel had become, to all appearance, a typical Fitzrovian *flâneur*; yet he remained, for all his efforts to detach himself from his inherited background, very much the callow and basically conventional young man with whom I used to travel daily from Blackheath to Cannon Street. Even his workman's clothes were not a very effectual disguise: indeed, by accentuating those plebeian traits which were part of his family inheritance, they made him look more of a Greene than ever.

As for his Communism, I felt pretty certain that it was precisely on a par with his romantic dedication to Art with a big A: a new phase, merely, in that life-long protest against authority which could be traced back to the tantrums of his childhood. The only odd thing about his conversion—seeing that Nigel had hitherto shown not the slightest interest in politics—was its suddenness: could it, I asked myself, have had anything to do with that glowing review, by the Marxist critic, which had so flatteringly hailed Nigel as an exponent of Socialist Realism?

The horrible Reg was another matter, and I found Nigel's attachment to him more and more puzzling. Reg, I decided, could hardly be explained in purely ideological terms, for, though suitably plebeian, he seemed notably lacking in enthusiasm for the Workers' Struggle against Fascism. Nor could I really believe that Nigel found him sexually attractive; for that matter, I had always thought Nigel's homosexuality a rather *voulu* affair, a kind of hangover from his schooldays which he had deliberately encouraged and exploited, partly from timidity where women were concerned, partly as an aspect of his protestant attitude towards his family and society in general. Homosexuality, like Communism, was fashionable among our contemporaries, and indeed for many of them (more especially the younger poets) was closely linked—by analogy, perhaps, with the Marxian synthesis of Theory and Practice—with the idea of left-wing solidarity and the breakdown of class barriers. Small wonder, then, that Nigel should have added this weapon to his armoury; but why, I asked myself yet again, should he have picked on Reg?

One evening, meeting Nigel in the Fitzroy, I was shocked to observe that he had a black eye and a long bloody scratch down the side of his cheek. This, I learnt, was the result of a "bit of a tussle"—as Nigel expressed it—with Reg. It was plain enough, in fact, that poor Nigel had been beaten up by his soul-mate, and plainer still that he had not in the least enjoyed it.

Later, I returned with him to the flat, where Reg gave vent, as was his habit, to a tirade of mocking abuse. Studying Nigel's face, I was reminded, suddenly, of an occasion many years ago, at The Grange, when he had sat as though spell-bound, watching his brother's performance upon the tennis court. Now as then, he seemed possessed by an emotion in which fear and hatred were strangely invested with the quality of some vicious obsession. It seemed a far cry indeed from the tennis lawn at The Grange, but I could guess that in Reg, the ex-soldier, boxer and gaolbird, Nigel had found a substitute for the brother whom he hated with a passion so oddly akin to love.

For all his assurances to the contrary, Nigel seemed to me to be plunged in a state of chronic misery; whatever obscure satisfaction he may have obtained from his masochistic idyll, it certainly hadn't made him any happier. I could guess that, in his heart, he longed to be back in the cosy, womb-like atmosphere of The Grange; instead, he was self-condemned to an indefinite sojourn in the hell of Howland Street, among the sardine tins, the unwashed glasses and the unsaleable pictures. The *époux infernal* showed no signs of relinquishing his functions, and the *vierge folle* seemed, by now, stoically resigned to his *saison en enfer*.

My own Season in Fitzrovia—an altogether more disengaged and frivolous one than poor Nigel's—came to an end at about this time, and Charlotte Street saw me no more. I remember that, at my last encounter with Nigel, he lectured me once again, very solemnly, about the Spanish War. He was seriously thinking, he said—despite his chronic prostatitis—of joining the International Brigade. Perhaps with this martial end in view, he had shaved off his beard, and was now growing a small and (so far) rather ineffectual moustache. He professed to be rather shocked by the fact that I was drinking bitter: he himself drank nothing but mild, being persuaded, it seemed, that the penny or so difference in the cost had great ideological significance—a point which, since I was a good deal poorer than he was, I found rather difficult to appreciate.

"Do you like winkles?" I asked him, suddenly remembering an occasion, years ago, when Nigel's ideology had been of a strikingly different complexion.

"*Winkles?*" he said irritably, annoyed by the apparent irrelevance of my question (Nigel, at this time, was very severe about what he called my "frivolous attitude").

"Yes, winkles. The shellfish, you know."

"Oh, I see. Yes, Reg often buys them off the stalls in the West India Dock Road—we go down there sometimes, one feels so much more *in touch* in the East End, you know. Though really," Nigel added, as an afterthought, "I rather prefer jellied eels myself."

In the summer of that year I spent several weeks in the south of France, staying first at Cassis, then at the Welcome Hotel at Villefranche. It was while I was at the Welcome that I received a postcard from Frankie, who wrote from an address in Jugoslavia; the card had been sent to Blackheath, and forwarded to me at Villefranche. I wrote to her at the address she gave, telling her where I was; a week later, much to my surprise, she turned up at the hotel, carrying a raffia bag which, it seemed, constituted the whole of her luggage.

"I've just walked here from Split," she announced, in the off-hand tones of one who has strolled from the Round Pond to the Achilles statue.

I was delighted to see her. When she had procured a room at the hotel and had a bath, she joined me on the terrace, and we proceeded to drink a great many *fines-à-l'eau* before dinner. Our conversation became decidedly uninhibited, and we talked a great deal of scandal, much to the embarrassment of a staid English couple who, somewhat incongruously, had chosen the Welcome Hotel for a quiet holiday.

"Who have you been rescuing lately?" I asked, for this had become a long-standing joke between us.

Frankie gave a fat little laugh.

"Oh, nobody much, really. There was a rather silly young German, who said he'd once met Isherwood in Berlin, so I put him up on a sofa for two nights, but then he went away, and I found he'd taken a nice little eighteenth-century watch that belonged to my mother."

"*I* think it's time you got married again," I said.

"Well, I've no particular objection, really, only I don't want another Harold" (this was her second husband, the drunken one), "he was always setting the house on fire, and the insurance people thought it was arson, but it was only because he would smoke in bed, poor lamb."

"We must find you some nice young man who doesn't smoke," I said.

"He'd be sure to do something else," said Frankie, with a comfortable fatalism. "Still, I agree, one does miss having a man about the house, they're so useful at parties, when people have to be chucked out."

After dinner, we wandered up into the town, and had some more drinks in the pubs and cafés. On our way back, about midnight, in one of the steep, narrow streets behind the hotel, we came upon what was apparently a corpse, spreadeagled upon the cobbles under a gas-lamp. Nobody was about, and I wasn't quite sure what we ought to do; as I pointed out to Frankie, if we went to the police, we might be arrested as accessories after the fact, the French police being notorious for such inconvenient *perversions de justice*.

Frankie, however, who had moved forward within the circle of lamplight, gave a sudden exclamation.

"He looks to me as if he were English," she said.

I followed her, and saw that the corpse was that of a tall, rather thin young man dressed in a tweed coat and flannel trousers. His face was turned away from me, and I bent forward to look at it.

"Good God," I exclaimed, "it's Nigel Greene."

Frankie had dropped to her knees, and was feeling his pulse.

"He's not dead," she said, "he's just passed out, I expect. He seems to have been bashed about a bit, but I don't think there's really much wrong with him."

Nigel's clothes were covered with mud, and there was a small wound on his forehead; he had either been knocked down or had tripped over the uneven cobble-stones and passed out on the spot. I went to a bistro which was still open, and got some brandy; Frankie had raised Nigel's head upon her knees, and we tried to perform that action so often described in adventure stories as "forcing the brandy between his lips". It proved no easy task, but after a time he began to show signs of life, moving his head to and fro and groaning. Suddenly he sat bolt-upright and was violently sick. It was another ten minutes before we could get him to his feet; probably he had been doped, for he stared at us with blank incomprehension, muttering vaguely to himself. I mentioned my name, but he obviously didn't recognize either myself or Frankie. There was no means of discovering where he was staying, so with considerable difficulty, supporting his wilting body between us, we at last got him back to the Welcome, where the night-porter rather reluctantly provided him with a bed; in order to obtain this favour, we had to explain that Nigel was *un artiste-peintre anglais très célèbre*, who had been eating bad shellfish—at which the porter, though he granted our request, looked sceptical, as well he might.

Between us, we got Nigel to bed, and Frankie dressed the wound on his forehead (fortunately her raffia bag contained, among other indispensable articles, a first-aid kit).

"Poor lamb, I expect he got beaten-up by some of those sailors," she said sympathetically (there was a British warship in port that night, and the bars had been crammed with ratings). "I'll pop down first thing in the morning and get the barman to make one of my special prairie oysters for him, poor sweet."

Frankie had the sort of look which I have often seen on the

faces of hospital nurses before a major operation: an expression of cool, business-like compassion. To anyone who knew her as well as I did, it was abundantly obvious that Nigel, whether he liked it or not, was going to be rescued at last, and with a firm hand.

Nigel, as it happened, when he had more or less come to himself—a process which took the best part of forty-eight hours—showed no rooted objection to being rescued. He had always been fond of Frankie, and was grateful, in a rather tetchy way, for her ministrations. We elicited his story in bits and pieces, two mornings after his installation at the Welcome; he had been staying at a small hotel along the port, from which we fetched his luggage as soon as he was able to remember the hotel's name. His notecase had been stolen, but fortunately he had left the bulk of his money, together with his passport and travellers' cheques, locked up in his suitcase. He had been with some sailors—French ones, not English, as it happened—in a pub, and thought he must have been drugged, for he remembered nothing more until he woke up at the Welcome to find Frankie bending over him with a prairie oyster, a cup of black coffee and a *Cachet Faivre*. Exactly what he had been doing in Villefranche and why he had come there at all, proved difficult to elucidate; from his confused ramblings it appeared that he had left England, originally, with the intention of going to Spain, but instead of taking the direct route had landed up at Marseilles, where he had been immediately arrested, though he could not—or would not—tell us exactly why. On his release, instead of going on to Spain and joining the International Brigade, he had decided, apparently, that he was not a Communist after all, but a Constructive Pacifist. This latest conversion had caused him (perhaps from some confused association of the idea of pacifism with Hindu philosophy) to turn east instead of west, and he had at last found himself at Villefranche. Suspecting that his sudden departure from England might have had some more personal motive, I asked after Reg, upon which Nigel burst into tears. It was no surprise to me to learn that Reg had vanished from Howland Street one night, while

Nigel was at a meeting, without a word of explanation, and taking with him every object of any value which the flat contained. A few weeks later, Nigel had learnt—possibly with mixed feelings—that the Child of Nature was now living with an elderly interior decorator in a flat off the Fulham Road.

A few days later Nigel departed, with Frankie, for England; she had decided to leave in any case, having heard sinister rumours about two Comrades whom she had left in charge of her house. Nigel seemed glad enough to accompany her; during the remainder of his stay at the Welcome he had remained sober, tractable and almost embarrassingly polite. Constructive Pacifism, I thought, seemed to be having a mellowing effect.

I remained, myself, for another ten days at Villefranche. Some weeks after my return home I was rung up by Frankie, who asked me to a small party to meet a Jugoslavian comrade whom she had picked up with at Split. I asked after Nigel, and was not altogether surprised to learn that he was now living in Frankie's house.

"I'll tell you all about that when I see you," said Frankie, in an off-hand tone, as though the topic rather bored her.

I arrived at the party somewhat early, to find only three or four people present. One of these was the comrade from Split, to whom I conversed for ten minutes in very bad French. Nigel was pouring out drinks, and looked not only much cleaner but a good deal happier than I had seen him for a long time, though he seemed, I thought, a bit subdued; I noticed that he was wearing one of his old tweed suits, his political allegiance being indicated, less obtrusively than in the Howland Street days, by a light red—almost a pink—tie. When I could escape from the comrade (whom I found a bore), I went up to him, and at the same moment Frankie joined us; we talked for a few minutes about Villefranche, then Frankie told me about all the trouble she had had with the two comrades who had been left in the house while she was away.

"Apparently they lived for a whole month on corned beef and Irish whisky," she informed me. "You should have seen the mess: tins and bottles piled up in every corner, and Jankl tried to hang himself one night in the bathroom, only fortunately Gyussi came in and found him just in time. Oh, by the way," she said, "I suppose you haven't heard—Nigel and I got married the other day."

She announced this astonishing fact in a casual, disengaged tone, rather as though she had just been to the Zoo or bought a new gramophone record. Nigel, too, seemed to take the change in his life very much for granted, and cut short my astonished congratulations to ask me whether I had read Huxley's *Ends and Means*. He was seriously thinking, I gathered, of taking up Yoga, inspired thereto by the writings of Messrs. Huxley and Heard.

"The important thing, you see, is the principle of *non-attachment*," he told me, with an air of great solemnity.

Our conversation was interrupted by the arrival of several comrades, Indian students from the London School of Economics; nor, during the course of the evening, did I have any further opportunity of getting either Nigel or Frankie to myself.

A week or two later, however, I met Frankie, by chance, in London, and we had lunch together at Bertorelli's. Though not exactly unwilling to talk about her latest marriage, she seemed to regard it as a topic of very minor interest; for her, I suppose, it was all in the day's work, and she was far more anxious to discuss a Mammoth Rally in support of the Popular Front which was to take place shortly at the Albert Hall. I wasn't in the least interested in Mammoth Rallies, and told her so; at last, with some reluctance, she was persuaded to give some account of her courtship, which had been conducted, apparently—as indeed I had suspected— entirely from her side.

"Poor sweet," said Frankie, through a mouthful of *spaghetti bolognese*, "he obviously needed looking after, and the house is much too big for me to live in by myself, so it seemed quite a sensible arrangement for both of us."

Frankie, it appeared, shortly after returning from Villefranche, had descended unexpectedly upon the flat in Howland Street, and had been appalled by its squalor and discomfort. Nigel had been in bed with a bad cold which seemed likely to turn to pleurisy; then and there, Frankie had ordered a car from the Daimler Hire

Company and carried Nigel off to Acacia Road, where she proceeded to "feed him up" for the next fortnight. At the end of this period Frankie had suggested that they might just as well get married, and Nigel, thus fattened for the sacrifice, had expressed no objection. Shortly afterwards the marriage had taken place, with a minimum of pomp, at a register office; though the occasion had been duly celebrated, the same evening, by a large party in Acacia Road, which had gone on well into the next day, somewhat to the scandal of the neighbours.

"I'd have asked you to it," Frankie explained apologetically, "only I knew you were out of town, and there really wasn't time to send out proper invitations. Nina got stinking—she took off all her clothes, and sang 'Ballocky Bill the Sailor'."

All this sounded quite the normal form; what did surprise me—and indeed made me choke over my spaghetti—was the astonishing news that the guests at this party had included Geoffrey and Madge. This I found so difficult to believe that I demanded to know full details, despite Frankie's evident desire to revert to her Mammoth Rally.

Geoffrey and Madge, it seemed, had happened to be in London on the day of the wedding, and Nigel had rung them up and invited them. Not only had they come to the party, but they had—if Frankie was to be believed—actually enjoyed it. Or at least, Geoffrey had; Madge had left rather early—she was staying with an aunt, with whom her husband was not on good terms, and Geoffrey had taken a room at a hotel.

"It was just as well Madge went when she did," Frankie continued. "She wouldn't drink more than one whisky, and I daresay she would have found Nina a bit unrefined."

I was so *bouleversé* by the mere thought of Madge and Nina being in the same room together, that I could only stare at Frankie speechlessly. Frankie's parties, it was true, did tend to operate as a powerful social solvent, she seemed able to entertain the most wildly disparate types without disaster either to them or to herself; but the reactions of Geoffrey and Madge, confronted by a roomful of long-haired artists and comrades of every conceivable race, class and sex, must (I thought) have put an abnormal strain upon even Frankie's powers of social orchestration.

Apparently, however, she hadn't batted an eyelid, and nor had anybody else.

"Geoff got as tight as a drum," said Frankie complacently. "He was rather a success, really, especially with the queers."

"Good God," I exploded, "I should have thought he'd have rushed round horse-whipping them all."

"Oh well, he hadn't got a horse-whip, for one thing," said Frankie reasonably, "and he was far too plastered to notice much. Actually, it was a fairly respectable party, to start with: Geoff seemed quite thrilled to meet Denzil Pryce-Foulger—Denzil came along with that dreary little Phipps man, you know who I mean."

"But good Lord," I exclaimed, "I remember Geoffrey reading Denzil's book, and saying he ought to be castrated."

"Oh well, it was a pretty ghastly book, you must admit."

"Yes, but whatever did they talk about—Geoff and Denzil, I mean?"

"Oh, rugger. They went on for ages, we couldn't stop them—I must say, Denzil's a crashing bore, especially when he's tight."

"Geoffrey *must* have been plastered," I said.

"Well, after all they were both rugger players, and anyway Denzil's married now—I forget who his wife is, but I know she's someone rather grand, so I suppose Geoff thinks Denzil's not queer any more. Not that *I* ever thought he was, really—it was just a pose, the same as Nigel." Frankie took a deep draught of Chianti, and added: "Actually, you know, I thought Geoff was really rather sweet."

"Did you really?" I said. The epithet was scarcely one I should have expected her—or indeed anybody else—to apply to Geoffrey.

"Yes, in that bristly, bulldoggy sort of way, you know. It's a pity he can't be got away from that dreary wife of his: they'd both be much happier if only she'd divorce him. She's a terrible snob, too—she was frightfully impressed when she heard my uncle was a lord, so Nigel told me."

Frankie said this with the faintest hint of complacence: proud though she was of being a "proletarian", I couldn't help feeling that she would be quite prepared, if some shift in the social pattern made it expedient, to boast of her maternal rather than of her paternal ancestry.

During the next few months, I saw Nigel and Frankie occasionally, though with decreasing frequency, for my health had not been good lately, and I found the parties at St. John's Wood more than I could cope with. So far as I could tell, the marriage seemed to be working out rather satisfactorily: apart from occasional parties, Nigel was being gradually weaned from his alcoholism, and a further course of prostatic massage, accompanied by the administration of the new sulpha drugs, had notably improved his health.

A change now occurred in my own life: in the spring of 1938 I left London and went to stay with my old nurse in the country. I lost touch almost entirely with most of my London friends, including Nigel and Frankie; the Greenes, indeed, became merged, in retrospect, into that vague, amorphous population of people I had once known—old schoolfellows, dim cousins and former friends at Oxford—but whom I wanted to know no longer.

My sole link with the Greenes, at this time, was through poor Molly who, from her self-imposed exile at Bournemouth, kept up a fitful though affectionate correspondence with my mother. She had never really recovered from "all that fuss" (as she called it) over Geoffrey, or from her husband's death, though the latter, one gathered, had been decidedly the lesser of two evils. She was in poor health, and very lonely; one of her eccentric cousins had died, the other had become a voluntary patient in a loony-bin. Molly had been once to stay with Geoffrey and Madge at Princes Risborough, but this, it seemed, had not been much of a success. "I know they don't really *want* me," she wrote, rather pathetically. Nigel's marriage seemed to have upset her less than one might have expected: Frankie, she confided to my mother, was rather "fast", but at least she was a lady. Doubtless her aristocratic connections went far to compensate, in Molly's eyes, for her shortcomings in other respects; for that matter (it occurred to me for the first time), Nigel's marriage had followed the Greene family tradition in being technically—if somewhat eccentrically—hypergamous.

It was just after Munich that, being in London for a few days, I ran unexpectedly into Geoffrey. He was having a drink in a pub called the Chandos, near Charing Cross; when I greeted him, he seemed scarcely to remember who I was. He spoke in a slurred, uncertain voice, and though it was only midday was already, quite obviously, half-drunk. He was still chicken-farming, he told me, but was thinking of returning to the Army; he remained on the Territorial Officers' Reserve, and seemed fairly confident of wangling some sort of job when the balloon went up, though probably not in his old regiment.

"Things have been a bit tricky, one way and another, since my spot of trouble," he said.

I asked after Nigel and Frankie: they were still living in Acacia Road, and Frankie—this came as a surprise—was very keen on Civil Defence.

"Nice girl, Frankie," Geoffrey added. "Knows some interesting people, too. Of course, all this Bolshy business is just a pose—Frankie's too much of a thoroughbred to take that sort of thing seriously."

Geoffrey, I thought, looked a lot older: his hair was receding from his forehead, and he was beginning to run to fat. Soon after our brief conversation, he left me, pleading an important engagement in the City.

A few months after this I had my last meeting—also quite fortuitous—with Nigel. For some reason which I forget, I was walking from South Kensington station towards Sloane Square, and had paused at the corner of Sloane Avenue to admire the Michelin building, to which I have always been much attached. As I stood looking at the frieze of coloured tiles, depicting scenes from Edwardian motoring days, I saw that a tall young man had also paused on the pavement edge, and was staring at the building with an interest as lively as my own. He wore a quite ordinary light-grey suit and a black hat; there was nothing in the least eccentric about him, he didn't look particularly arty or particularly conventional, he might have been an advertising copy-writer or something to do with films. Then he happened to turn in my direction, and I saw that it was Nigel.

The encounter had a curiously dim, unemphatic quality about it: Nigel himself seemed to have become in some way diminished, neutralized, a person who had ceased to be quite real.

We greeted each other friendlily enough, though I felt with Nigel, as I had with his brother, that it required an effort on his part to recognize me. "Isn't it *appalling*?" he said, looking at the Michelin building, and seemed astonished when I replied that, on the contrary, I thought it delightful. As a matter of fact, the presence of Nigel added point to my rather specialized *culte*, for the Michelin building evoked for me much the same atmosphere—breezy, up-to-date and self-consciously twentieth century—as Geoffrey's old house at Wrotham. I pointed out this perhaps rather over-subtilized parallel to Nigel, who looked entirely baffled.

"Four Winds?" he echoed, at a loss. "But surely that was *Tudor*?"

He glared at me dubiously through his horn-rimmed spectacles; he looked, I thought, cleaner and in general more "presentable" (as my family would have put it) than at any time since I had known him.

I asked after Geoffrey.

"Oh he buffles along—he's a frightful drunkard, nowadays," said Nigel primly. "The chicken-farm's gone down the drain, apparently: Geoff's rather hoping to get a job in the R.A.S.C., if there's really a war."

"Do you think there's going to be a war?" I asked, not because I valued Nigel's opinion, but rather from curiosity as to what ideological position he had now assumed.

"Oh, I don't think so, do you? They couldn't possibly afford it," he asserted. "I read something in the *News Chronicle* the other day which said that all their tanks were made of cardboard."

"What will you do if there *is* a war?" I asked.

"Well, actually," he said, looking at me shyly, though with a touch of his old nervous defiance, "I'm thinking of joining the Territorials, as it happens. Geoff's pretty keen on it, you know, and it does seem rather a good thing at the moment."

"But I thought you were a pacifist," I said.

Nigel blinked at me, vaguely.

"Oh well, yes, of course I am really," he said. "But I'm medically unfit, you see—it's my eyes, chiefly—so they'd shove me in the Pay Corps or the R.A.M.C., probably."

I asked after Frankie, and learnt that plans were afoot—in the event of war—for turning the house in Acacia Road into a very progressive and left-wing canteen for A.R.P. workers. As we talked, the bleak winter twilight deepened: it was half-past four, with an hour to go till opening time, or I might have suggested a drink. As it was, we soon parted: Nigel was on his way to a meeting of Czech comrades, I was bound for some other and more frivolous destination.

I watched Nigel slouch away down the darkening street towards South Kensington; as his tall, gangling figure receded, it seemed to me as though "the street were time and he at the end of the street", and I turned away towards Sloane Square, with a sense that another phase in my life had come to an end.

It was late in 1939, after the war had started, that I saw in *The Times* the announcement of Molly's death—"peacefully, at Bournemouth". Our letters of condolence were sent to Geoffrey, but it was Oonagh who replied, explaining that her brother was already on active service with the R.A.S.C. She wrote a polite, characterless letter, in her small, neat handwriting, thanking us for what she called our "floral tributes". Reading between the lines, one could infer that poor Molly had gone slightly dotty, as she had always expected; she had spent her last months in a nursing home, but nobody had realized how ill she really was, and she had in fact died of an inoperable cancer. Nigel, as well as Geoffrey, joined with her (said Oonagh) in thanking us; but she didn't say what Nigel was doing, or where he was.

Calypso's Isle

Gozo was charming: a smaller yet somehow more spacious and less claustrophobic version of Malta itself. Colonialism had touched it, but touched it lightly, and as I looked from my top-floor window in John Causton's house I felt, for almost the first time since I had left England, that I was genuinely abroad. The house stood on a slight eminence, just to the north of Rabat, the capital town, and from here one's eyes swept the entire island, from shore to shore. In the soft, honey-coloured evening light, the long parched fields swept gently upward to ridge or hilltop, each little hillock crowned, inevitably, by the bubble-dome of a huge baroque church. There must, I thought, be more churches to the square mile in Gozo than anywhere else in the world; yet this land, surely, was irredeemably pagan, the Madonnas enshrined beneath those swelling, maternal domes were no Christian goddesses, but Demeter or Cybele; and the nymph Calypso lingered yet, perhaps, in her cave at Ramla, luring the unwary traveller to linger on her shores.

The late sunlight faded as I unpacked my bag, the fields lapsed into darkness, and the lights shone out in the town nearby. Downstairs, dinner was laid on the terrace, beneath a pergola heavy with gourds and clusters of purple grapes.

"You're nearly late," my host informed me, with a touch of sharpness. "Another two minutes and the *pasta* would have been over-cooked: it must be *al dente*, the Maltese are quite hopeless, it's something one can never teach them. Help yourself to a drink while I dish it up."

John Causton was an old acquaintance of mine, whom I had once known fairly well; nowadays, however, our reunions tended to be infrequent, for he had adopted an increasingly nomadic way of life, settling first in Greece, then in Alexandria and later in Sicily. Gozo he considered to be his own particular discovery, and he was a trifle snobbish about it, assuming a proprietary air towards its beauties, like Mme Verdurin at La Raspelière. A pleasing though not very enterprising painter, he possessed a small private income, and was able to maintain an air of amused detachment towards the world in general which I found enviable.

"I've concocted a rather good *sugo*," he said, popping his head in from the kitchen. "Oil, *peperoni*, black olives and just a touch of basil. I shall hate you if you don't adore it."

A moment later the bowl of steaming *pasta* was placed on the table. It was a delightful dinner, especially after the horrible food in Valetta; the spaghetti was followed by aubergines stuffed with rice and minced chicken, and these by a salad; before the meal was over, we had drunk several litres of Chianti.

In appearance, John reminded one irresistibly of Lytton Strachey: thin, bearded, his sharp eyes concealed by dark spectacles. To those who didn't know him well, his air of aloofness was apt to suggest that he was permanently rapt in a trance of creative activity; nothing, in fact, could have been further from the truth, for he was passionately and incessantly absorbed in the social life around him, and was by nature a good old-fashioned gossip who could be relied upon to nose out, with an uncanny rapidity, all the juiciest and most incriminating scandals endemic in any place which he happened, at the moment, to be inhabiting.

"And now," he said, having opened the second bottle of wine, "I want to hear everything, but *everything*, about Mervyn: does he still give those terrible parties in Islington, and who goes to them, and have you been yourself?"

Mervyn Huw-Williams was a rather successful pianist known to us both; his private life—more especially in its erotic aspects—was a source of immense and perennial interest to those who could claim the somewhat dubious honour of his acquaintance. I supplied such details as I could about Mervyn and other people whom we knew; then it was John's turn, and I realized that he was really much less interested in the *mœurs* of Bohemian London than in what was going on within a few yards of his own doorstep. Some of his tales were, indeed, so scabrous as to make the activities of Mr. Huw-Williams seem positively humdrum by comparison.

It was not until the coffee was on the table that it occurred to me to ask him whether, by any chance, he had come across a man called Tufnell-Greene.

"*That* old monster—how in the world did you manage to pick *him* up?"

I related briefly the story of my encounter at the hotel in Valetta, adding that Geoffrey was a distant relation of mine.

"Oh well, every family has a skeleton in its cupboard, we know that, but really how *extraordinary*. He's the prize bore of the archipelago, we run miles to avoid him, but *miles*. I'm sorry to cast aspersions on the gentility of your family, but I'd better tell you at once that he's widely known as the Not-so-pukka-sahib. Mind you, I hardly know him myself, but from what one *hears*— and I do hear quite a lot in my *tour d'ivoire*, though you mightn't think it—he sounds positively the end: madly snobbish, but can't quite make the grade, and his wife's worse, I'm told, really she's terrible, always telling everyone how well-connected she is, and making coy little jokes about toilets and taking sugar in one's tea."

I was sorry to hear that poor Madge had become so silly, but I had always suspected her of snobbish aspirations, and these were no doubt easier to gratify in Malta than at Princes Risborough or even Wrotham.

"The trouble with Not-so-pukka," John went on, "is that he boozes like a fish and can't take it. He gets maudlin, so I'm told, and then passes out, and Little Woman has to bustle round putting him to bed, so tiresome for her."

Madge, I thought, would hardly find this rôle a very sympathetic one, and said as much to John.

"Oh, she's very efficient, apparently. Mind you, she can drink her husband under the table, any night: I don't know where she learnt her boozing habits, but she can certainly put it back."

"But she used to be practically a teetotaller," I said, with astonishment.

"Well, she's not now, I assure you."

In my time, I had seen the Mediterranean climate work wonders on the most intractable material; but I found it difficult to believe that Madge, of all people, should have succumbed.

"Don't they live at Mdina?" I said, remembering that the hall-porter at the hotel in Valetta had said something to this effect.

"Oh yes, a rather pretty little baroque house, I believe, though I've never been inside it. I suppose they get quite a good rent for it in the summer, but I must say we *do* all wish they'd stay there, instead of coming over and corrupting the Gozitans."

"But *do* they come over?" I said.

John raised his eyebrows.

"But my dear, I thought you *knew:* they have a cottage just down the road, on the way to Xlendi."

"Are they there now?"

"Are they not—I saw the Colonel's lady only this morning, buying soap-flakes in Ik-tokk. What did you say her name was—Madge? I always call her Calypso, myself—she keeps the wily Odysseus pretty firmly at anchor, I suspect, while they're over here, though he's a bit too wily for her on occasion. I saw him in Valetta about a month ago, getting properly sozzled with a bunch of Cameron Highlanders. It's funny," John added ruminatively, "that he should be Bert Greene's brother: come to think of it, *he* must be your cousin, too. What a literary family you are."

"*Bert* Greene?" I exclaimed.

"Yes, *you* know—the one who wrote *The Taste of Human Flesh*."

"But *that* wasn't Geoffrey's brother," I said.

"I assure you it was."

"But Geoffrey's brother was called Nigel, and anyway it couldn't possibly have been the same person. Why, I've known Nigel all my life, he was a painter of sorts, he certainly never wrote a book." Suddenly I remembered the mysterious remarks of the hall-porter in the hotel at Valetta. "There *must* be some mistake," I added.

"It's really quite true," John insisted. "It seems odd you shouldn't have known, seeing that he was your cousin."

"As a matter of fact," I said, "I've never read the book, but I do remember Bert Greene, vaguely, in *New Writing* and *Horizon*, during the war—rather bad stories about the Army."

"Oh yes, *those*—but he didn't really have any success till *The Taste of Human Flesh*. It caused quite a stir at the time, if you remember: I thought it rather drear, myself, but lots of people boosted it, including Cyril."

I did remember the title as that of a rather sensational novel which I had missed at the time of publication, and had subsequently failed to catch up with. Yet I found it impossible to believe that Nigel had written a book which had been praised by Cyril Connolly, and of which I had remained all but unaware.

"But what *sort* of book is it?" I asked helplessly.

"Oh, autobiographical, I suppose," said John. "Nasty, brutish and short, so far as I can remember—its brevity was about the best thing in its favour. Not really *me*, at all, but it certainly had more *réclame* than one would have expected. Not-so-pukka positively dines out on it to this day, I'm told—or at least, Calypso does. The burra sahib's slightly peeved, one gathers, at being presented somewhat unflatteringly."

"But why *Bert* Greene?" I asked.

John shrugged his shoulders; and then, suddenly, I remembered that the horrible Reg, Nigel's "Child of Nature", had been accustomed to call Nigel "Bert". For that matter, I thought, it had been common enough for left-wing middle-class writers to assume such monosyllabic and plebeian *noms de guerre* at that period.

"Oh well, if you won't believe me," said John at length, "I believe I've got a copy of it somewhere—it was done in Pans or Penguins, and I bought it to read in the plane coming out. I must say, I can understand your getting confused—there are such a lot of literary Greenes, aren't there? Graham, Henry, F. L., G. F., Peter, Julien—one just doesn't know where one is."

He disappeared into the house, and shortly returned with a paper-back edition of the book. I glanced at it sceptically, and turned to the title-page: THE TASTE OF HUMAN FLESH, by Bert Greene. "For information about the author," said a note on the fly-leaf, "see back flap." I turned to the back flap, and was confronted by the photograph of an emaciated, bearded person who did, it was true, look something like Nigel in his Howland Street days. My eyes fell to the enclosed square of letterpress below the picture, headed "About the Author", and which read as follows:

"Bert Greene (Nigel Herbert Tufnell-Greene) was born at Blackheath in 1907. He was educated at Uppingham, and worked in his youth with an insurance firm; he also studied, for a time, at the Goldsmith School of Art at New Cross, and in 1936 held a one-man show at the Wertheimer Gallery; several of his pictures are now in private collections. Early in the last war, he enlisted in the Army, and served for three years in the Pay Corps. In 1943, while stationed at Malta, he sustained serious injuries as a result of enemy action; he made a partial recovery, but his health rapidly worsened, and he died on the island of Gozo in May 1947. His first book was *Roll on Christmas* (1945), a collection of short stories dealing with Army life, some of which had previously appeared in *Horizon, New Writing, Bugle Blast*, etc. Two short excerpts from the present novel were printed in *Orpheus* and *Orion*; the book was completed just before the author's death, and appeared, posthumously, in 1948."

There were the facts, set down in cold print, and I could no longer doubt them. Yet how had I remained so totally unaware of Nigel's brief—though apparently successful—career as a writer? True, I vaguely remembered the stories of Army life in the little magazines, but they had left scarcely any impression upon me. How had I managed to miss the novel? I glanced once again at the date of first publication: 1948. As it happened, I had been in the Army during most of that year, and had been kept far too busy to bother much about new books. I did just remember reading reviews of *The Taste of Human Flesh*, but they had provided no clue to the author's identity. Odder still seemed the fact that I had seen no announcement of Nigel's death: I looked at the blurb again—he had died in May 1947, and I now remembered that I had spent the spring and early summer of that year in Italy, where I certainly hadn't bothered to look at the *Times* or the *Telegraph*.

I glanced over the "quotes" from reviews which were printed on the fly-leaf of the book. "A searing human document", said the *Daily Mail*; "new, vital, exciting", was the verdict of the *Birmingham Post*. *Time and Tide*, less forcefully but with quiet conviction, asserted that Mr. Greene's was "one of the few major talents to emerge from the war". In the *Sunday Times*, Nigel was compared with Henry Miller: "the most revealing book of its kind that I have read since Miller's *Tropics*".

That Nigel's celebrity should have been posthumous struck me as having an ironic appropriateness: it was difficult, somehow, to imagine the living Nigel in the rôle of successful author.

Reading Nigel's novel was for me a disquieting, almost an eerie experience: not because of the book's intrinsic qualities, but because, as I read it, I seemed to be listening to the living voice of the writer. It is never easy, at the best of times, to be wholly impartial about books by people one knows, and in this case I found it difficult to remain even moderately detached. Try as I might to pretend that I was reading the novel of a total stranger, there was no mistaking that tone of exacerbated defiance, those passages of shrill invective which, here and there, rose to the literary equivalent of a scream. The style was turgid, exclamatory and cliché-ridden, yet it had a sort of hysterical vitality which made the book—for all its faults—compulsively readable. It was, in fact, the sort of novel which makes literary criticism look silly: it *ought* to have been bad, and indeed, judged by any ordinary standards, it *was* bad; yet it succeeded in creating precisely the effect which the writer had, presumably, intended. Nigel, as I could guess, had taken to writing just as, in earlier days, he had taken to painting or music, in a mood of reckless, untutored enthusiasm; but this time, by a miracle, he had managed to bring it off.

The book was, as John had said, fairly short, and I read about half of it in bed that night, finishing it after breakfast the next morning. It was, of course, autobiographical: names were changed—Greenes became Brownes, they lived at Hampstead instead of Blackheath—but in all essentials Nigel had stuck fairly closely to the facts. His parents, Geoffrey, Oonagh and various Greene relations were all perfectly recognizable, so were their houses, though Nigel hadn't much talent for characterization, still less for conveying the particular atmosphere of The Grange or of Four Winds. Primarily, the novel was a study of Nigel's relationship with Geoffrey ("Kenneth" in the book), and the strange mingling of love and hatred, hero-worship and contempt, which Nigel had felt for his brother, and of which I had long been dimly aware, was extraordinarily well suggested.

There were several rather juicy descriptions of beatings: in one of the earlier of these I had no difficulty in recognizing the episode which had taken place in our garden at Sandgate. The title of the book derived, as it happened, from this incident: Nigel, in biting his brother's wrist, had been simultaneously thrilled and disgusted by the "taste of human flesh", and the memory of this was made to recur, with a haunting persistence, throughout the novel. Much later, when he was about fourteen, Nigel had been caught out in a lie, and Geoffrey had given him a dozen of the best across the bare buttocks; on this occasion, Nigel had had an orgasm—the first of his waking life—and had been terrified. Afterwards, the matter was never again referred to, and this was the last of Geoffrey's beatings, though he would occasionally treat Nigel to solemn and minatory lectures about the dangers of masturbation.

An account of Nigel's schooldays followed: homosexual episodes at Uppingham in which, oddly enough, the love-object was in most cases not an older boy, as one might have expected, but one younger than himself. It was as though Nigel, at this stage, wanted to identify himself with his brother, and to reproduce the relationship in reverse (I remembered the choir-boy at All Saints'). Nigel's time at the insurance office was mentioned only in passing, and from Uppingham the narrative skipped to the Goldsmith School and Fitzrovia; there were squalid affairs with prostitutes, and an abortive episode with a young man, a fellow-student at the Goldsmith.

Nigel's attack of gonorrhoea was described with a wealth of intimate and humiliating detail; the book ended, rather abruptly, with the departure of Reg from Howland Street, and there was no reference to Frankie, or to Nigel's marriage.

Such were the bare outlines; but the real point of the book was its complete and devastating exposure of a self-confessed humbug. It was, in fact, an all-too successful essay in psychological strip-tease, and at the end of it Nigel was left morally naked, without a shred of self-respect to cover him. His painting, his politics, even his sexual life, were exposed as so many *personae*, fake attitudes which had been assumed to conceal the pitiful inadequacy of his real self. He had, for instance, felt a perfectly normal attraction towards women, but an innate timidity—reinforced by his "dose"—had made him adopt a homosexual rôle which, as I had more than half suspected, was almost wholly fictitious. The affair with Reg was analysed with a brutal candour; no less savage was Nigel's debunking of his own artistic pretensions, and the most hostile of critics could not have condemned his pictures with a more vitriolic malice than did Nigel himself.

Nigel, if anything, was inclined to over-emphasize his own failings, but his portrait of Geoffrey was, by contrast (I thought), ever so slightly sentimentalized. In the earlier sections of the book, at any rate, "Kenneth" was portrayed on altogether too heroic a scale, though in the later chapters, as though to offset this, Nigel was free with his hints that Geoffrey's sexual life was less orthodox than might have been supposed; not content with retailing various details about Geoffrey's mistresses, he actually accused him of homosexual practices—an invention which could only, I thought, be attributed to sheer malice (or perhaps wishful-thinking) on Nigel's part. So far as one could tell, it was his sole excursion into pure fiction.

Not even his worst enemy, I thought (laying down the book, at last, among the breakfast coffee-cups), could have exposed Nigel's falsity and pretentiousness more ruthlessly than he himself had done in this extraordinary testament. His capacity for self-deception had, as he frankly admitted, been all but inexhaustible, making it

143

only too easy for him to regard even the most squalid and humiliating episodes in his career in a romantic and self-flattering light. Then, one must suppose, had come the moment of truth—probably as a sequel to the war-wound which had crippled him—and this book had been the result.

Nigel's life, from childhood onwards, had been a series of protests, most of them pathetically ineffectual: from the first he had fought a losing battle, the big guns were all on the other side. *The Taste of Human Flesh* was, so to speak, Nigel's atom bomb—exploded belatedly, in the latest phase of his private war, but none the less effective by contrast with those conventional weapons which had previously constituted his feeble and inadequate armament.

Nigel's novel was, I supposed, a triumph of Art over Life: the whole of his drab, unhappy, frustrated career had reached its culmination in this single book, and was perhaps—as some might think—thereby justified. But was it? The ruthless self-dedication of a Flaubert, Joyce's proud, penurious exile—these were all very well; but "Bert Greene" was no Flaubert, or Joyce either. Could a minor work such as this—and minor it was, though certainly remarkable—justify, *sub specie aeternitatis*, the follies and miseries of a life such as Nigel's had been? I doubted it; yet the fact remained that, from the dead wood of his discredited phantasies and his delusive ambitions, he had been able to create a work of art which, though crude and ill-executed, was in some respects unique. Thirty years ago I had been inclined—much as I might distrust his pretentious assumption of the rôle of "artist"—to give Nigel the benefit of the doubt; it was better, I had thought, even to pay lip-service to Art than to despise or ignore it; and perhaps, after all, I had been right.

John was obliged to work that morning: he was busy, as he apologetically explained, sketching out the designs for a series of murals which had been commissioned (on extremely profitable terms) by a rich Maltese businessman.

"If you want to bathe," he said, "I should go down to Xlendi bay—it's the nicest beach, and the nearest. And who knows," he added mischievously, "you might run across your not-so-pukka cousin."

It was arranged that John should follow me, in one of the cheap Gozitan taxis, after his morning's work, and take me home to a late lunch. He pointed out the direction, and I set off through the hot, brilliant morning. Half-way down the hill towards Xlendi, I noticed a little white box of a house, standing back from the road behind a hedge of prickly pear, which—from John's description—I recognized as being the home of Geoffrey and Madge.

Another ten minutes' walk brought me to Xlendi itself: a single row of fishermen's cottages, a pub and a little restaurant, strung out along a small bay rather like a Cornish cove. There was a sandy beach and, below the cliffs on the eastern side of the bay, a line of flattened rocks admirably adapted for sunbathing. In front of the pub, tables and chairs were disposed invitingly beneath the shade of a row of tamarisks. It was extremely hot; I strolled leisurely along the deserted quay, and made my way towards the flat rocks on the farther side of the beach. From the doorway of the Calypso Bar a girl of haunting beauty smiled at me as I passed. Here, surely (I thought), was the true Ogygia, "remote from the track of ships", a fitting haunt for that nymph or goddess in whose power it lay to bestow the gift of eternal youth.

I bathed from the rocks, in the deep water of the bay, then lay roasting in the fierce mid-morning sun. I dozed for half an hour or so, for we had been late to bed last night; when I awoke, the empty landscape had suddenly become populous: a party of British soldiers, in camp on the hillside above the village, had invaded the beach, and were shouting and splashing in the shallows. A few, more enterprising, had swum farther out, and their voices carried clearly across the smooth, landlocked waters: shouts of animal laughter, facetious comments bawled out in Cockney or Lancashire accents. With their bronzed, muscular bodies, they seemed a part of this classic landscape, Homeric heroes lured by the nymph to the Ogygian shore. Suddenly I caught sight of a tall, beefy figure in bathing-trunks descending the steps on to the beach, opposite the Calypso Bar: none other than the wily Odysseus himself, in the incarnation proposed by John Causton; a rather podgy but still quite personable hero whom I knew by the name of Geoffrey Greene. I saw him stop and speak to a group of soldiers who were lounging against the wall below the steps; at last, with a self-conscious little flounce, he turned away from his companions, sprinted down the beach and took a running dive into the sea. He swam out strongly across the bay towards where I was sitting, and for the next twenty minutes or so I observed him as he splashed, swam or supinely floated some thirty yards from shore. His body was burnt to the colour of mahogany; as he floated in the calm water, I could see his stomach rising like a brown, burnished dome above the level of his torso—the "bit of pot" which, when he had talked to me in the hotel bar, he had so much deplored.

Since our last encounter, he had acquired a new interest for me: I saw him, as it were, through Nigel's eyes—or, more accurately, through the eyes of the narrator in Nigel's novel. Who would have supposed that anybody—let alone Nigel—would ever put Geoffrey into a book? Yet now, in this pot-bellied elderly man, puffing and blowing in the water below me, I was bound to recognize the heroic yet sinister figure of "Kenneth" in *The Taste of Human Flesh*.

Geoffrey at length swam ashore, and not long after I returned to my rock and dressed. When I arrived at the Calypso, a few minutes later, I found him sitting beneath the tamarisks on the terrace, with a large whisky-and-soda in front of him, and looking rather less than Homeric. He wore his alpaca coat and a coloured sweat-rag inside his open shirt-collar; he looked very conscious of being an English gentleman properly dressed for the beach, and glanced, I thought, with a shade of disapproval at my T-shirt and rather grubby flannel trousers.

"Good morning, it's Geoffrey Tufnell-Greene, isn't it?" I said.

He glared at me blankly.

"Sorry, old boy—I'm afraid you have the advantage."

"We met in Valetta, you know, two nights ago. You had to dash off rather suddenly, if you remember. I owe you a drink, as a matter of fact."

Geoffrey frowned at me, bewildered and rather suspicious.

"I can't say I—oh yes, I do remember having a drink with a chap, come to think of it. Early in the evening, eh?" He gave a sudden burst of laughter. "To tell you the honest truth, I don't remember an awful lot about that night. Fact is, I'd had a few before I met you, and after that I had to go and meet someone down at the docks—my son, as a matter of fact, in for the night, you know. I got invited on board his ship, and—well, quite frankly, I'm buggered if I know how I got off it." He gave another bellow of laughter, then glanced at me more closely. "Why, of course," he said, "you're the bloke that wouldn't put on his coat."

"D'you remember my saying I thought we'd met before, somewhere?"

Once again I saw suspicion gleam in his eyes.

"Can't say I remember that," he said, rather sharply. "Don't even remember your name."

"I didn't remember yours till the page called it out, and you'd gone the next minute." I told him my own name, adding, "We're sort of cousins, you know."

It was a moment or two before the penny dropped.

"Just a second, what did you say your name was?"

I repeated it.

"Why, good God yes, of course I remember you now. Your people lived in Blackheath Park, didn't they, when we were at The Grange?"

"Yes, that's right—we used to live at Sandgate, before that."

"Good Lord, yes—it all comes back: you were a friend of Nigel's, weren't you? Look here, old man, you must forgive me, the fact is I've a rotten memory for faces, and it's—well, it must be a fair number of years since we met, eh? You've changed quite a bit, too, if you don't mind my saying so."

"I suppose that happens to all of us, after twenty years."

"Your mother still alive? And your brother Cecil?"

I explained that my brother had died in the war.

"Oh Lord, I'm sorry about that—he was a damned decent scout . . . Fact is, you know, one loses touch—the war, and one thing and another . . . Well, this is the most extraordinary thing: what are you drinking, by the way?"

"It's my turn, really."

"Never mind about that—I'll have the next one with you."

I asked for a Bitter Campari.

"What, that Eyetie stuff? No, no, have a decent drink, for God's sake."

I was in no mood to argue, and accepted a brandy—a large one, since Geoffrey insisted.

"And you may as well bring one for my wife," he said to the beautiful girl whom I had seen earlier. "She'll be down in a few minutes. And another whisky for me: that'll be two large brandies, one large whisky—got it, Teresa?"

"How is Madge keeping?" I asked, realizing that I had not yet inquired after her. I couldn't help feeling some surprise, in spite of what John had told me, that she was in the habit of drinking double brandies before lunch.

"Madge?" For some reason Geoffrey seemed surprised by my question, and once again his face had a blank, baffled look. "Oh, Madge is all right, from all I hear. Tony—that's my lad, you know—spent his embarkation leave with her. She's got a house at Littlebourne, near where her father used to live, in Kent. Tony tells me she's taken to breeding chinchillas—jolly little beasts, he says they are."

"But I thought she was here," I exclaimed, totally bewildered.

"Thought she was *here*—who, Madge?"

"You just ordered her a drink."

Geoffrey stared at me with a bewilderment equalling my own.

"What the hell—oh Lord, I thought you realized." He sank back, with a deflated air, into his chair, and gave a short, embarrassed laugh. "The fact is, you see, Madge isn't my wife any more. I'm—er—well, as it happens, I'm married to Frankie."

"To *Frankie*?" I gasped, dumbfounded. "Frankie Cartwright?"

"Well, Frankie Greene, as she was when I married her. She was married to Nigel, you know." Geoffrey buried his nose in his whisky. "Fact is, Madge and I got a divorce back in forty-eight. I'd no idea you didn't know—no reason why you should, of course, after all I hadn't heard about your brother. Funny how one loses touch . . . I let Madge divorce me, naturally: there was no difficulty, I was living with Frankie by then, you see." He eyed me cautiously over the top of his glass. "Things were never the same, you know, after my spot of trouble. We'd have got a divorce before, if it hadn't been for the children, but once they were grown-up, it didn't seem to matter. Madge and I have always kept on good terms, though—after all, she's a—" I thought he was going to say a "lady" or a "gentlewoman"; he paused, however, and added "a thoroughbred".

"It was nice seeing Tony," he went on, his manner becoming less constrained. "If I could raise the fare, I wouldn't mind hopping over to Cyprus and looking him up. He's hoping for his third pip any time now. Gwen's doing well, too—she's going in for this ballet-dancing, you know, Tony thinks she may land a job at Sadlers' Wells."

It was a moment before I remembered that Gwen was the name of Geoffrey's daughter.

"It's really jolly extraordinary we should meet up here," he went on. "Frankie'll be thrilled to death—she was talking about you only the other day."

"Talking about *me*?" I said in surprise.

"Yes—didn't you write a book, or something?"

I admitted that this was the case.

"Well, Frankie had been reading it, and it made her laugh quite a lot. We live rather out of the world here, you know, never get any news to speak of, and Frankie was wondering what had happened to you. I'm afraid," he added, apologetically, "I didn't read the book myself—I don't seem to get much time for reading, these days. We didn't realize that you'd blossomed out as an author."

I thought this a good opportunity to explain that, until last night, I had been in precisely the same position with regard to Nigel.

I saw Geoffrey's face go taut with embarrassment.

"Oh yes, he did write a book—it was a long time ago, of course, I thought most people had forgotten it by now."

I explained, once more, how I had come to miss the book myself, and said how sorry I had been to hear of Nigel's death.

"I suppose you heard about his—er—I mean, how he died?" Geoffrey muttered.

"Only what I read on the back of the book, I'm afraid," I said. Seeing the waitress passing near our table, I ordered more drinks. When these had arrived, I encouraged Geoffrey to continue.

"It was out here in Malta, you see. Nigel got posted here, in the Pay Corps, near Valetta. A shell got him at close quarters—he was damned nearly killed outright. As it was, he lived for another four years: extraordinary thing, really—the doctors were amazed at the way he seemed to pull himself together. He was a cripple, of course—paralysed all down one side, and bad internal injuries. His—er—pelvis and all that were smashed up too, it was about as ghastly as it could be, dead from the waist down, if you get me."

Geoffrey looked at me with a horrified disgust in which, I thought, there was a curious touch of prudishness.

I could think of nothing to say.

"It was an awful business in every way," he went on. "I was in the Middle East, Benghazi way, couldn't get any leave, though, things were sticky just then, and it was all stopped, even compassionate. Frankie got out to him, as soon as they'd let her—there was quite a bit of wire-pulling, I guess. They managed to wangle his discharge without taking him back to the U.K.—he'd have probably died on the voyage, anyway. Frankie got him over here, and found a house—the one we're in now, just up the hill—and they stayed there till he—till Nigel packed up." Geoffrey took a gulp of whisky. "I will say this," he continued, "Nigel was really bloody courageous. It sounds a pretty awful thing to say about one's own brother, but I—I'd never have thought he had it in him. Pulled himself together in a wonderful way—in fact, I sometimes think those last few years were the happiest of his life."

"And that was when he wrote—" I was going to mention the book's title, but something made me avoid it, and say instead "—his novel?"

"Yes, he slogged away at his writing all the time." Avoiding my eyes, as he bent to light his pipe, he said: "Have you read it, by the way—that book he wrote?"

I said that I had, adding—for the sake of saying something—that it had had an extremely good press.

"Yes, I gathered that it was pretty well thought of, in some quarters," said Geoffrey, still occupied with his pipe. "Mind you, I'm not literary, that sort of stuff's frankly beyond me, I suppose I'm too stupid. I could barely get through the book myself, it didn't seem to have any story—a good thriller's more in my line. You're literary, of course, I don't expect you to agree, but I thought it an awful load of balls."

I guessed that Geoffrey, from the first, had decided to brazen out the business of Nigel's novel as best he could; his plain-blunt-soldier pose had, I thought, the ease of long practice, and I couldn't help admiring his performance.

"But I must say," Geoffrey repeated, raising his eyes and regarding me with a soldierly frankness, "I do take off my hat to him: he was damned brave to buckle to as he did, and make the best of things."

No epitaph, I thought, could have pleased Nigel more. I wondered if he had ever realized, in those last years, that he had finally justified himself in Geoffrey's eyes; but this I was never to know.

The rest of the story was rather slurred over: Geoffrey, demobilized, had come to visit Frankie twice during Nigel's illness, and after his death had stayed on for a couple of months. So much he told me: the rest I could imagine—Geoffrey at a loose end, drinking heavily, with enough money to live on, but hopelessly estranged from Madge, and dreading the return to Princes Risborough. He had turned to Frankie, whom he had always (rather surprisingly) liked; and Frankie, obeying the dictates of her nature for the fifth—and presumably the last—time, had proceeded thereupon to rescue him, just as she had rescued Nigel and his three predecessors.

"Well, never mind all that," Geoffrey exclaimed briskly, after a longish silence. "You're ready for another drink. Where are you staying, by the way?"

"I'm staying with a friend of mine—his name's John Causton."

"Oh, that fellow—an artist, isn't he—chap with a beard?"

"Yes, that's the one."

Geoffrey gave a nod.

"I've seen him around—met him at one or two parties, that sort of thing. Can't say I know him, really. Frankie's met him too . . . Look here, now," he broke off, "I was just trying to work out how you and I were related: as far as I can remember, my grandfather must have married a great-aunt of yours, isn't that it?"

"He married two of my great-aunts, as it happens," I said, without much interest. Geoffrey, however, seemed determined to explore every aspect of our relationship, and we were still engaged in this—to me—boring exercise, when Frankie arrived.

"Oh, hullo," she said, as casually as if we had last met twenty-four hours rather than twenty years ago, "we were just talking about you the other day, and I was wondering where you were living."

I don't think that, if I had met her in the street, I should have known her: the hall-porter at the Valetta hotel had described Geoffrey's wife—mistakenly, as I had supposed—as "stoutish", but this epithet, applied to Frankie, was an understatement. She had grown immensely fat, and it was with difficulty that I recognized, half-buried as they were beneath a vast acreage of circumambient flesh, the placid, rather cat-like features which I remembered.

"Oh, John Causton," she said, when Geoffrey had told her with whom I was staying. "I've met him, of course, but I don't really know him at all well. We're rather cagey in Gozo, you know, it's just like an English village, people tend to 'keep themselves *to* themselves'." She took a long drink of brandy, and added, "You must come to dinner, and bring John: what about tomorrow?"

I said that I should have to ask John, who was rather busy. At

152

that moment, as it happened, John himself arrived in the taxi from Rabat, Geoffrey ordered more drinks, and the party took on an air of heightened conviviality. I had been slightly nervous, after John's disobliging remarks on the previous night, of this encounter with the Greenes; as it happened, I need not have worried, for John, as was his habit with people whom he disliked or mistrusted, had plainly decided to exert his charm, which on such occasions could be considerable. Soon he and Frankie were deep in local gossip, and for the next few minutes I was rather left out of the conversation, which dealt in rapid succession with innumerable Maltese and Gozitan personalities whom I didn't know.

"I must say, I think Betty's a perfect dear," I heard Frankie saying. "The way she lives in open sin with Tom, and in the middle of Mdina, too. The fact is, of course, that people accept her just because she *is* so nice."

"And also, possibly, because she's fairly grand," John suggested. "An Hon. still goes a long way in Malta, you know. I must say, *I've* always had a soft spot for her, though I really prefer her sister Charmian."

"Oh, do you know her?" said Frankie, with a casualness which was just a little overdone: I could see that she was, in fact, much impressed.

"Charmian's an old and dear friend of mine," John replied calmly. "She's one of the few women I might have married—we did have serious thoughts of it, at one time."

This I knew to be perfectly true; I also knew that Charmian was an extremely smart and fashionable woman, one of the famous débutantes of the early thirties, daughter of a rich lord and married to a still richer oil-magnate. Her sister, Betty, according to John, was considered by her family to be hopelessly *déclassée*, besides being a terrible bore.

"I did meet Charmian's husband once ages ago, I thought he was a sweetie," said Frankie, but this gambit fell rather flat; John was obviously winning on points.

I wondered why he should bother to play this particular game, though it was evident that he found it amusing. The truth was, I thought, that John, though fond of condemning snobbery in others, was something of a snob himself, but in parenthesis, as it were; I had once, indeed, heard him confess that he liked to know who was who, in order to tell snobbish people who was not.

"I hear the Smith-Vassalos were wild at not being asked to Betty's party," he now remarked.

"Oh, they're terrible snobs, aren't they?" Frankie exclaimed, with a laugh. "If it comes to that, Betty herself can be fairly U-conscious on occasion—she gets furious with poor Tom because he will call their drawing-room the lounge. It's all frightfully silly, of course, but some things do rather grate on one, don't you find?"

At this point Geoffrey, who like myself had been feeling rather out of things, unexpectedly chipped in.

"Why the hell *shouldn't* he call it a lounge, if it *is* one?" he asked irritably.

"Oh but Geoff, darling, one just doesn't, that's all," Frankie replied, with a cosy little laugh.

At this moment, John turned away to order more drinks, and I shifted my chair nearer to Geoffrey's. I felt rather sorry for him: was he, I wondered, pining for Ithaca?

"I remember the lounge at Four Winds perfectly well," I said tactfully. "It was panelled, and the front door led straight into it, like a sort of hall—the kind of room that people *do* call a lounge."

Geoffrey looked at me gratefully.

"Yes, that's right," he said, "you couldn't really call it a drawing-room, not like the one at The Grange, for instance. It was rather a jolly house, Four Winds, wasn't it? Decent country, too—I never really took to Princes Risborough. D'you remember that pub we used to go to—the King's Arms?"

"Yes, of course I do."

"Nice little place, the chap who kept it had good taste, didn't spoil it like they're doing nowadays. There's nothing like a real country pub, is there? The beer was good, too, at the King's Arms. God Almighty," Geoffrey exclaimed, with a sudden burst of nostalgia, "I'd give my eyes to be in a real English pub at this moment, with a dirty big pint of bitter in front of me."

He fell silent, listening with an aggrieved air to John and Frankie, who were still absorbed in social niceties. As for myself, I found Frankie's snobbery both amusing and rather saddening: it was a far cry, I thought, from the "comrades" of the thirties, the mammoth rallies and the parties in Acacia Road.

At last John looked at his watch, and gave a small shriek.

"D'you realize it's two o'clock, and I haven't bathed yet? Look here," he said, turning to me, "would you absolutely loathe it if we had something to eat down here? The food's filthy, but I promise to cook you a delicious dinner tonight, and I was only going to have omelettes for luncheon, anyway."

The taxi was dismissed, we lunched in the little restaurant, and the rest of that afternoon passed in a daze of sun and alcohol. After lunch we all bathed again, with the exception of Geoffrey, who went to sleep under a tamarisk; he seemed grumpy and looked, I thought, a little pale beneath his tan. At five o'clock the Smith-Vassalos arrived: the friends of Frankie whom she had described as being such "terrible snobs". Their snobbery, I noticed, didn't preclude Frankie from greeting them with every sign of affection. More drinks appeared, and the Smith-Vassalos asked us all to dinner in two days' time; John and I were to dine with Geoffrey and Frankie tomorrow.

It was seven o'clock before we managed to get away; by the time we left we were all very drunk, not least so Geoffrey, who became slightly lachrymose, and began to talk to me again, incoherently, about Four Winds.

"It's a lucky thing for Not-so-pukka that he has the mem-sahib to look after him," said John, on our way home. "Incidentally, I thought you said her name was Madge, or Gladys, or something?"

I explained my mistake, and gave a brief account of my former relations with her.

"I hadn't the faintest idea she'd been married to Bert Greene," John confessed. "You see what an ivory tower I live in . . . I suppose he needed mothering, like Not-so-pukka."

"Frankie's a great one for rescuing the fallen," I explained.

"Well, I quite see that she'd be terribly good at it. I do adore that nice, motherly kind of Lizzie, so cosy, don't you find? I always fall for them like mad."

"If you're not careful," I said, "she'll be rescuing *you*, next."

Next morning, as was to be expected, I had an appalling hangover; even John, more habituated than myself to the rigours of Gozitan conviviality, confessed to feeling a little off-colour.

A Fernet Branca and two benzedrine tablets revived me sufficiently to face the prospect of a bathe; John decided to take the day off, and we drove over, with a picnic lunch, to the land-locked bay of Kawra. After lunch and an hour's sleep, I felt a great deal better, and we proceeded to hold a post-mortem on the events of the previous day. John demanded to know full details of Frankie's various marriages and about her past life in general; we laughed a good deal over her activities in the thirties, and the recent striking change in her ideological outlook.

"It's extraordinary," said John, "how many people one knows, of about our age, who are still trying to live down the thirties. Look at Mervyn, for instance: Aid for Spain, and hunger marches, and that dreary chum of his—a welder or a fitter, or something, from Barnsley, or was it Burslem?—and now he's so grand he'll hardly know us, flaunting around with his bowler and his rolled umbrella, and telling everyone how he danced with Princess Margaret. Not but what he still doesn't have his rough-stuff, but at least he doesn't have to be ideological about it."

"He was never very ideological about women, even in the thirties," I pointed out.

"No, but I bet Frankie was. Honestly, you know, I did enjoy teasing her—I must try and think of a few more solecisms she doesn't know, before tonight."

"Tonight?"

"Yes, we were asked to dinner, don't tell me you've forgotten."

"I honestly don't think I can face it," I groaned.

"Oh yes you can, don't be so lily-livered, we'll go to a place in Ik-tokk where they have real pre-war absinthe, and you'll feel fine. It's funny, you know," he went on, pursuing his earlier train of thought, "how snobbery has gone to people's heads since the war, just like sex did in the twenties. In the old days, things like milk-in-first and calling looking-glasses mirrors just weren't mentioned, any more than French letters or sanitary towels. And now of course we've all become frightfully frank and outspoken, though it's still a little daring, you know, especially for people like Frankie, who were madly left in the thirties. Did you notice, yesterday, how positively reckless she looked, when we were talking about it? I daresay her mother looked just the same when she mentioned wombs or lavatories."

The pre-war absinthe in Ik-tokk completed my cure, and at eight o'clock we walked unhurriedly down the hill, through the warm darkness, towards Xlendi. Geoffrey was waiting to welcome us outside his small white house, and almost before we were through the door was offering us enormous glasses of brandy. Presently Frankie appeared from the kitchen, and we were taken for a tour of the house. The sitting-room produced, upon myself, a curiously dream-like effect: I recognized several pieces of furniture from Acacia Road, and others which I remembered from The Grange or Four Winds. The walls were hung with Frankie's pictures, and some of Nigel's—one of these, showing two all-in wrestlers clinched in a rather suggestive pose, had been shown at the Wertheimer Gallery, and had afterwards hung in Nigel's flat in Howland Street. Seeing me pause in front of it, Geoffrey remarked, rather to my surprise, that he thought it "jolly life-like".

"Makes you feel as if you were in the ring yourself," he said, pointing at the strained, distorted body of one of the wrestlers. "If you ask me, Nigel ought to have stuck to painting."

I was reminded of Geoffrey's father showing me his Bouguereaus and Henners at The Grange, thirty years ago.

"I daresay you remember that one, don't you?" he said, pointing to a small picture over the mantelpiece which I hadn't noticed.

It was the little Boudin—a wedding-present from old Mr. Greene—which had hung, unregarded, in a corner of the "lounge" at Four Winds.

"Madge wasn't terribly keen on it, you see," Geoffrey explained, "so I thought I might as well have it myself. It was about the only thing I did take, of any value, when we—when I came out here. I was always rather fond of it."

The picture was a sunlit, windy seascape of Trouville or Dieppe; I found Geoffrey's attachment to it oddly touching. His taste, I thought, was a good deal better than his father's.

Soon our glasses were liberally refilled, and I began to feel slightly muzzy; the mixture of brandy and pre-war absinthe was perhaps, I thought, a mistake.

Just how great a mistake it had been, I was not to realize, fully, till the following morning. Meanwhile, I allowed Geoffrey to refill my glass without protest; by the time dinner was ready, we had drunk several large brandies, each equivalent, I suppose, to a double if not a treble tot. The dinner, when at last it occurred, was excellent—Frankie had always been a good cook—though I was hardly in a state, by now, to appreciate it. Indeed, I remember little more about that evening; we must all have been fairly drunk, but for some reason John—who usually had a good head—became very drunk indeed: so much so, that Frankie—much to her satisfaction—was compelled to perform rescue operations. The patient was firmly dosed with Eno's, and put to bed; I myself was in no condition to walk up the hill to Rabat, and was accommodated on a mattress in the sitting-room.

I was awoken the next morning by Frankie appearing with her time-honoured remedies: black coffee and prairie oysters. Struggling painfully back to consciousness, aware that I was only half-undressed, seeing Frankie and the familiar pictures, I had, once again, a feeling that time had telescoped itself. It was just like old times in Acacia Road, I thought, half-expecting, as I glanced round me, to see half-a-dozen recumbent comrades disposed about the room.

That night we dined with the Smith-Vassalos, and during the next week or so parties proliferated; during the day, while John was working, I spent most of my time on the beach at Xlendi.

Frankie was usually occupied, until after midday, by domestic affairs, but Geoffrey would arrive regularly at about half-past ten or eleven, and we would bathe or sit on the rocks until, as he said, the sun was over the yard-arm, which meant twelve o'clock (Geoffrey was a great stickler for alcoholic etiquette, and would never drink anything before midday). We became, during those long, hot mornings, increasingly friendly; Geoffrey, it is true, was inclined to be glum and snappish before he had had a drink, but a whisky or two at the Calypso rapidly revived him. He had, I decided, mellowed with age, and was now almost likeable. At first he was rather shy, and spoke as little as possible; later, he became slightly more loquacious, though his talk was of a desultory kind, coming in fits and starts, as though he were thinking aloud. Often he would sit for half an hour at a time, gazing silently out to sea, or watching the soldiers as they splashed in the shallows or played games with a medicine-ball upon the beach.

On one occasion he was thrilled by the arrival of a party of West Kents, to whom he stood drinks all round.

"Fine lot of chaps, aren't they?" he said, as we sat on the parapet, watching the brown, muscular bodies crowding the beach; and I saw his eyes light up, as he spoke, with a nostalgic enthusiasm.

Once, when the sun was well over the yard-arm, and Frankie had not yet arrived, he became more than usually confidential.

"The fact is," he said, "I'm fed up with the life out here: it's cheap enough, and the climate's good, but I'd give a lot to get back to England and settle in the country somewhere. When you get down to brass tacks, there's really nowhere like England."

"Why *don't* you go back?" I asked.

He gave me a quick, evasive look, and turned away.

"Oh no, it wouldn't do, it wouldn't do," he muttered.

I said nothing, but wondered—as I had wondered before—why Geoffrey should choose to immure himself in a place which he so obviously disliked. His "spot of trouble" must have been long since forgotten, and there seemed no other reason for his exile.

Suddenly, as though pursuing some parallel train of thought, he began to speak, in a vague and circuitous way, about Nigel.

"You know," he said, with a shy, sidelong glance at me, "you might not believe it, but I was pretty fond of Nigel. We hadn't much in common, of course, and I daresay I used to knock him around quite a bit, when he was a kid, but he was frightfully spoilt, and I only did what I thought was right."

I should have liked to ask what he really thought of Nigel's novel, but decided that the subject was best avoided.

"Actually, you know," he continued, musingly, "it's a pity he didn't go into the Army sooner, when he was younger; it might have been the making of him."

Geoffrey's eyes were fixed upon a detachment of the Duke of Wellington's Regiment who had just fallen in, after a bathing-parade, opposite the Calypso bar. As he spoke, he ran his hand—it was a way he had—caressingly over his naked shoulders, his chest and his rather protuberant belly, as though he were stroking a cat.

Oddly enough, I was inclined to agree with his last remark: Nigel, I thought, was the sort of person who needed some sort of framework for his life, and the Army might have provided it.

"Pity he had to die," said Geoffrey, after a long pause, adding rather sadly: "There aren't so many of the family left, you know, nowadays—the Greenes seem to be dying out."

It occurred to me to ask after Oonagh.

"Oh, she's still down in Essex, you know," Geoffrey said, without much interest. "I saw her when I went over last time: she'd got frightfully fat. Her husband's doing rather well with that farm of his—fruit and vegetables, mostly, they sell their stuff to the canning factories."

One morning, when I was expecting him, Geoffrey didn't turn up. Instead, Frankie arrived about midday, explaining that Geoffrey was "not so well".

I was surprised to hear this, and asked what was wrong.

"Oh, he's got a dicky heart, you know," said Frankie. "He'll be all right in a day or two, he just needs a rest. The trouble is, he will overdo it: it's not the booze so much—though he ought to lay off that, too—it's all this swimming, and rushing about in general.

There's not much wrong, actually, but the doctors say he ought to take things easy for a few months, only of course he won't."

We bathed, then went to the Calypso and had some drinks.

"Geoff practically drove me out of the house," she said. "He can't stand being fussed over, and he said you'd be wondering where he was. Christina's there, anyway" (Christina was the Greenes' indigenous maid-of-all-work), "she'll give him his lunch. I rather thought I'd have something down here."

I had planned to do the same, and we lunched together. It was almost the first time, since my arrival, that I had had her to myself; on the first of October, she told me, they were returning to Mdina, having let the cottage at Xlendi, for the winter, to two English painters.

"Such funny little men, like gnomes," she said. "But we asked an enormous rent, and they fell for it, they must be quite rich."

Presently, after a bottle or two of wine, I plucked up courage to ask Frankie what Geoffrey had really thought of *The Taste of Human Flesh*.

"Oh well, he was rather difficult at first: I had to let him see it in manuscript, and he made me cut out one or two bits; but after that he became quite amenable, really. And when the book came out, and got such good notices, he was rather thrilled, though he pretended not to be."

Frankie had drunk quite a lot of wine by now, and I ordered some more.

"I must say, I'm surprised he took it so well," I said, "considering the things Nigel said about him. It was a bit much, making Geoff out to be queer. Wasn't he furious?"

"Well, of course, he didn't much like it, but as I told him, it was true anyway, and nobody cares a hoot nowadays, so then he gave way."

I was just refilling Frankie's glass, and in my astonishment slopped the wine on the tablecloth.

"But you don't mean to tell me that Geoffrey's *really* queer?" I exclaimed.

"Oh Lord, yes, didn't you realize? He's always been bi, I suppose, without knowing it. That's what used to make him so frightfully anti, I expect—latent queers always get angrier about it than anyone else, haven't you noticed? Geoff still thinks it's awfully wicked, actually—he gets dreadful guilt-feelings whenever he has anybody."

"But *does* he—have people?"

"Oh yes, sometimes, when he gets plastered. That's why we live out here, really—Geoff would love to get back to England, but he's scared, after all those prosecutions."

"But how did you—I mean, when did he really find out about himself?"

"Well, he didn't really *do* anything till the war, at least I don't think so, though I remember he came to a party of mine, and got quite gay with Denzil Pryce-Foulger."

"But you don't mean that he and Denzil——"

"Oh no, but he'd read Denzil's book and I suppose meeting Denzil and a lot of other queers sort of set him thinking. Then he was in the Middle East in the war, and he had an affair with some young man in the desert: they were sleeping in the same tent, and it was awfully hot, and it just happened, and after that he couldn't stop."

I could only stare incredulously at Frankie.

"Poor Geoff was in a dreadful state before we got married," she went on. "He felt he had to tell me all about it, it was quite embarrassing really, he kept saying what a filthy swine he was, and how I must despise him. As if *I* should mind," Frankie giggled, helping herself to more wine.

"I still can't really believe it," I said.

"Well, it's quite true, I assure you. It's funny, when you come to think of it, that Geoff should have been really queer, and Nigel never was properly, though he liked people to think so."

I was aware, as I had been on more than one occasion since my last night in Malta, of a sense of shifting frontiers, of fixed categories becoming merged into an amorphous, dream-like unity.

Presently I asked Frankie a few questions about Nigel's last years, a subject upon which she tended to be somewhat reticent. One significant fact did, however, emerge: Nigel, during his illness, had become deeply religious, and had died, it seemed, fortified by the comforts of the Anglo-Catholic Church. This, I thought, added a rather disappointingly conventional coda to the tale of Nigel's career; yet, remembering All Saints', Blackheath, I was bound to admit that it had been implicit in the thematic material of the earlier movements.

Geoffrey and Frankie returned to Mdina on the first of October. Geoffrey seemed perfectly recovered, and during the days before he left was swimming as energetically as ever. On the night before their departure, they gave a farewell party; the rains had started that day, and the guests, whom Frankie had hoped to entertain in the garden, were packed uncomfortably into the sitting-room. There was hardly room to stand up, and it was unbearably hot.

The two painters who were taking the house for the winter had turned up: both of them bald, fortyish and with fluting Cambridge accents; as Frankie had said, they were just like two little gnomes.

One of them expressed his interest in Nigel's picture of the all-in wrestlers.

"It's so *just* what one would expect from his book, isn't it? I suppose you've read it, haven't you? Really a *wonderful* novel—it haunts me, positively haunts me, and it's years now since I first read it. How extraordinary that Geoffrey Greene should be the *brother*—we had no idea till Frankie told us, and now we want to hear all about him, but *all*. I suppose *you* didn't know him, did you?"

I said that at one time I had known Bert Greene rather well.

"You *did?*" he exclaimed excitedly. "But do tell me what he was *like?*"

"To tell you the truth," I said, "I always found him rather a bore."

The little man looked taken aback: for him, evidently, Nigel's name had already become legendary.

"One thinks of him as having been such a *marvellous* person," he said piously. "So sensitive, yet so enormously *vital*."

Unwilling though I was to discourage the birth of so promising a myth, I felt compelled to say that Nigel hadn't struck me as being either vital or particularly sensitive.

"Oh, but I'm sure if you'd really *known* him—" he peered at me, with a mildly accusing air, through his spectacles. "It seems," he went on, "they take him *tremendously* seriously in the States. Laurie—my *friend*, you know—was over there last year, and a friend of his at Ohio University's writing a thesis on Bert Greene for his Ph.D."

I stayed on in Gozo for another fortnight; most of the English and Anglo-Maltese families had departed with the coming of the rains, and I had Xlendi Bay almost to myself. After a few days' downpour, the fine weather returned; the sun was still hot, the sea warm as milk, and I spent my days bathing and lazily exploring the adjacent cliffs which, after the rain, were suddenly covered with a transient, spring-like vegetation—patches of bright green grass, starred with tiny white narcissus. The Calypso Bar would shortly be closing down for the winter: the proprietor was only waiting until John, myself and the few other habitués had consumed his stock. He had long since run out of Campari, whisky and brandy; we were reduced, now, to gin and the very nasty local wine. The soldiers came no longer; an elegiac atmosphere prevailed, one was sadly aware of summer's lease expiring, and of the approach of winter. I felt, obscurely, that it was not only the end of the season, but the end, so far as I was concerned, of an epoch: I was nearly fifty, and the coming winter became identified, in my mind, with the melancholy prospect of old age and impotence.

I swam about in the deserted bay, and climbed the cliffs, collecting bulbs of the little narcissus for a botanical friend in England. At last even the gin ran out at the Calypso, and my money seemed likely, at any moment, to do the same. I said good-bye to John with a curious sense of finality: somehow I didn't think I should ever return to this island. I crossed the straits in the little steamer, spent a night in the hotel where I had met Geoffrey, and flew to England on the following morning.

*

It was not more than three months afterwards that I saw, in *The Times*, the announcement of Geoffrey's death—"suddenly, at Mdina, Malta, G.C." I heard later, from Frankie, that it had been a coronary thrombosis: poor Geoffrey had collapsed in some bar in the town and never recovered consciousness.

Almost exactly a year later I noticed another announcement in *The Times*—this time among the marriages.

"CAUSTON: TUFNELL-GREENE" (it read)—"On February 14th, 1958, at Valetta, Malta, G.C., John Edward Causton, elder son of the late Lieut.-Colonel and the Hon. Mrs. Alan Causton, to Francesca ('Frankie') Tufnell-Greene (*née* Poynton)."

So Frankie had rescued John after all. It was not, I thought, a matter for any great surprise, and it seemed likely that they would suit one another rather well. I sent John a letter of congratulation, but had no reply: he had always been an extremely bad correspondent. Some months later, however, I heard from Frankie who, though she sounded as serene and cheerful as ever, complained that she and John were finding it hard to make ends meet. On Geoffrey's death, his income had reverted—by an arrangement made at the time of his divorce—to the children of his first wife. The cost of living, even in Malta, had trebled or quadrupled during the last ten years, and the combined resources of John and Frankie were scarcely adequate to keep them in comfort. Frankie, therefore, had decided to turn their house at Mdina into a small and select convalescent home for British officers.

Nothing, I thought, could have been more suitable; though I was inclined to suspect that Frankie's motives, in embarking upon this laudable enterprise, were less purely economic than her letter might lead one to suppose.